Helen Hunt Jackson

Bits of Talk, in Verse and Prose, for Young Folks

Helen Hunt Jackson

Bits of Talk, in Verse and Prose, for Young Folks

ISBN/EAN: 9783744770606

Printed in Europe, USA, Canada, Australia, Japan

Cover: Foto ©Andreas Hilbeck / pixelio.de

More available books at **www.hansebooks.com**

ST. CHRISTOPHER. — PAGE 7.

IN VERSE AND PROSE,

FOR YOUNG FOLKS.

By H. H.,

AUTHOR OF "BITS OF TALK ABOUT HOME MATTERS,"
"BITS OF TRAVEL," "VERSES."

"—— in all the lands
No such morning-glory."

BOSTON:
ROBERTS BROTHERS.
1876.

CONTENTS.

CONTENTS.

BITS OF TALK.

THE PARABLE OF ST. CHRISTOPHER.

To a king's court a giant came, —
　"O king, both far and near
I seek," he said, "the greatest king,
　And thou art he, I hear.

" If it please thee, I will abide;
　To thee my knee shall bend;
Only unto the greatest kings
　Can giants condescend."

Right glad the king the giant took
　Into his service then,
For since Goliath's mighty days
　No man so big was seen.

Well pleased the giant, too, to serve
　The greatest king on earth;
He served him well, in peace, in war,
　In sorrow, and in mirth,

Till came a wandering minstrel by,
　　One day, who played and sang
Wild songs, through which the devil's name
　　Profanely, loudly rang.

Astonished then the giant saw
　　The king look sore afraid;
At mention of the devil's name,
　　The cross's sign he made.

" How now, my master!　Why dost thou
　　Make on thy breast this sign?"
He said.　" It is a spell," replied
　　The king — " a spell divine,

" Which shall the devil circumvent,
　　And keep me safe and whole
From all the wicked arts he tries
　　To slay my precious soul."

" O, ho, my master! then he is
　　More powerful than thou!
They lied who called thee greatest king;
　　I leave thy service now,

" And seek the devil; him will I
   My master call henceforth,"
The giant cried, and strode away
   Contemptuous and wroth.

He found the devil soon. I ween
   The devil waited near,
Well pleased to have this mighty man
   Within his ranks appear.

They journeyed on full many a day,
   And now the giant deemed
At last he had a master found,
   Who was the king he seemed.

But lo! one day they came apace
   To where four roadways met,
And at the meeting of the roads
   A cross of stone was set.

The devil trembled and fell back,
   And said, " We go around."
" Now tell me," fierce the giant cried,
   " Why fearest thou this ground ?"

The devil would not answer. "Then
   I leave thee, master mine,"
The giant said. "Of something wrong
   This mystery is sign."

Then answered him the fiend, ashamed:
   " 'Twas there Christ Jesus died;
Wherever stands a cross like that,
   I may not, dare not bide."

" Ho, ho !" the giant cried again,
   Surprised again, perplexed;
" Then Jesus is the greatest king,—
   I seek and serve him next."

The king named Jesus, far and near,
   The weary giant sought ;
His name was everywhere proclaimed,
   His image sold and bought,

His power vaunted, and his laws
   Upheld by sword and fire;
But him the giant sought in vain,
   Until he cried in ire,

One winter eve, as late he came
  Upon a hermit's cell:
" Now by my troth, tell me, good saint,
  Where doth thy master dwell ?

" For I have sought him far and wide,
  By leagues of land and sea;
I seek to be his servant true,
  In honest fealty.

" I have such strength as kings desire,
  State to their state to lend;
But only to the greatest king
  Can giants condescend."

Then said the hermit, pale and wan:
  " Oh, giant man! indeed
The King thou seekest doth all kings
  In glorious power exceed;

" But they who see him face to face,
  In full communion clear,
Crowned with his kingdom's splendor bright,
  Must buy the vision dear.

" Dwell here, O brother, and thy lot
  With ours contented cast,
And first, that flesh be well subdued,
  For days and nights thou'lt fast ! "

" I fast ! " the giant cried, amazed.
  " Good saint, I'll no such thing.
My strength would fail; without that, I
  Were fit to serve no king ! "

" Then thou must pray," the hermit said ;
  " We kneel on yonder stone,
And tell these beads, and for each bead
  A prayer, one by one."

The giant flung the beads away,
  Laughing in scornful pride,
" I will not wear my knees on stones ;
  I know no prayers," he cried.

Then said the hermit, " Giant, since
  Thou canst not fast nor pray,
I know not if our Master will
  Save thee some other way.

" But go down to yon river deep,
　　Where pilgrims daily sink,
　And build for thee a little hut
　　Close on the river's brink,

" And carry travellers back and forth
　　Across the raging stream;
　Perchance this service to our King
　　A worthy one will seem."

" Now that is good," the giant cried;
　　" That work I understand;
　A joyous task 'twill be to bear
　　Poor souls from land to land,

" Who, but for me, would sink and drown.
　　Good saint, thou hast at length
　Made mention of a work which is
　　Fit for a giant's strength."

For many a year, in lowly hut,
　　The giant dwelt content
　Upon the bank, and back and forth
　　Across the stream he went,

And on his giant shoulders bore
   All travellers who came,
By night, by day, or rich or poor,
   All in King Jesus' name.

But much he doubted if the King
   His work would note or know,
And often with a weary heart
   He waded to and fro.

One night, as wrapped in sleep he lay,
   He sudden heard a call:
" Oh, Christopher, come carry me!"
   He sprang, looked out, but all

Was dark and silent on the shore.
   " It must be that I dreamed,"
He said, and laid him down again;
   But instantly there seemed

Again the feeble, distant cry:
   " Oh, come and carry me!"
Again he sprang, and looked; again
   No living thing could see.

The third time came the plaintive voice,
　　Like infant's soft and weak;
With lantern strode the giant forth,
　　More carefully to seek.

Down on the bank a little child
　　He found, — a piteous sight, —
Who, weeping, earnestly implored
　　To cross that very night.

With gruff good-will he picked him up,
　　And on his neck to ride,
He tossed him, as men play with babes,
　　And plunged into the tide.

But as the water closed around
　　His knees, the infant's weight
Grew heavier and heavier,
　　Until it was so great

The giant scarce could stand upright;
　　His staff shook in his hand,
His mighty knees bent under him,
　　He barely reached the land,

And, staggering, set the infant down,
　And turned to scan his face;
When, lo! he saw a halo bright
　Which lit up all the place.

Then Christopher fell down afraid
　At marvel of the thing,
And dreamed not that it was the face
　Of Jesus Christ, his King,

Until the infant spoke, and said:
　" Oh, Christopher, behold!
I am the Lord whom thou hast served!
　Rise up, be glad and bold!

" For I have seen and noted well
　Thy works of charity;
And that thou art my servant good,
　A token thou shalt see.

" Plant firmly here upon this bank
　Thy stalwart staff of pine,
And it shall blossom and bear fruit,
　This very hour, in sign." .

Then, vanishing, the infant smiled.
   The giant, left alone,
Saw on the bank, with luscious dates,
   His stout pine staff bent down.

For many a year, St. Christopher
   Served God in many a land;
And master painters drew his face,
   With loving heart and hand,

On altar fronts and church's walls;
   And peasants used to say,
To look on good St. Christopher
   Brought luck for all the day.

I think the lesson is as good
   To-day as it was then —
As good to us called Christians
   As to the heathen men:

The lesson of St. Christopher,
   Who spent his strength for others,
And saved his soul by working hard
   To help and save his brothers!

2

A CHRISTMAS-TREE FOR CATS.

WHEN I was a little girl, I knew two old maids who were so jolly and nice that I am always ready, beforehand, to love anybody who is called an old maid. To be sure I have never yet seen any others in the least like them; and I begin to be afraid that that particular kind of old maid has died out, like the big birds called Dodos, which used to live in Australia. But I am always hoping to see two more before I die, and that I shall find them living together in a pretty little yellow cottage, just like the one the Miss Ferrys lived in, and that they will keep four splendid cats, just like the cats the Miss Ferrys had. I never saw such cats. Nobody ever saw such cats. They were almost twice as large as common cats.

Miss Esther Ferry used to say that if there was anything in the world she utterly despised the sight of, it was a little dwarf of a cat; and as soon as she began to talk about it, her black cat Tom used to stand right up and bulge himself until all the hairs of his fur stood out like the spokes of a wheel. Tom was the cleverest cat of the four. He really did understand more than half of all that was said before him, and sometimes Miss Esther used to send him out of the room when the neighbors were telling her any gossiping story. "Of course I know that Tom can't repeat it," she would say; " but it does make me nervous to have him listen so, and he is just as well off down cellar." Tom and Spitfire were Miss Esther's cats; we thought they were a little handsomer than Spunk and Yellow, who belonged to Miss Jane; but I think it was only because we loved Miss Esther best that we

thought so. Strangers never could decide
which of the four cats was the best looking.
Tom was as black as ink, — not a white or
gray hair about him; Spitfire was a Maltese,
of the loveliest soft mouse color all over,
with a great white star on her breast; Spunk
was pure white, and her eyes shone like
topazes in the sunlight; Yellow was a tor-
toise-shell cat, black and yellow and white:
he was the largest and fiercest of the four.
We were all more afraid of him than of any
dog in town. You will hardly believe it,
but these cats used to sit in high chairs at
the table, and feed themselves with their
paws like squirrels. They had little tin
plates, with their names stamped on them;
and one of the things I used to like best to
do, when I went there to tea, was to change
their plates, and then watch to see what
they would do. Yellow was the only one
who would eat out of any plate but his

own; he was always greedy, and did not care. But the others would look down at the plate, smell of it, and begin to mew; and once black Tom jumped right across the table at Spunk, who had his plate, pushed her out of her chair, and dragged the plate away. It was some minutes before he would let her come back to the table without spitting at her. But the best time we ever had in that dear yellow cottage was at a Christmas party which the old ladies gave for their cats. I don't believe there was ever such a thing heard of before or since. I knew about it a week before it came off, and it was the hardest secret I ever had to keep. My mamma came home one evening just at dark. I was lying on a sofa in a dark corner, where she could not see me, and papa was sitting by the fire. She went up to his chair and kissed him, and burst out into such a laugh, as she said, "Darling, what do you suppose those dear absurd old Ferrys are going to do? They are going to have a Christmas-tree for their cats."

"You are not in earnest, Mary," said papa.

"But I am, though," said mamma, sitting down on his knee, and putting her arms around his neck. It makes the tears come into my eyes even now, to remember how my papa and mamma used to love each other. Since I have grown up, and have seen what men and women really are, I know how wonderful it was. They have been in heaven a great many years, but it would be hard to make me believe they are very much happier there than they were here.

"But I am. You always think I am joking."

"Because you always are," interrupted papa.

"Don't interrupt. You are always interrupting," said mamma. "I have been at the Ferrys' for an hour this afternoon, and the dear old souls are quite beside themselves about it. They are going to have linen drilling put down over their carpets, and they are wondering whether it will do to have as many as twenty cats in the room with twenty children."

"The old geese!" exclaimed papa, who was not always quite as civil as he could be.

"I don't know," said mamma thoughtfully. "I am not so sure about that. I think it will be great fun; and Helen will be out of her senses."

I could not keep still any longer. I bounded off the sofa, crying, "O mamma, mamma, am I really to go? And shall I take Midge?"

Midge was my cat, a dowdy little gray

cat, whom nobody ever called **good-looking,** but whom **I** loved dearly.

"Mercy on me!" screamed mamma. "How you frightened me! You bad child, to lie still, and hear secrets. But you will be punished enough by having to keep one for a week. You must not tell a soul. Nobody knows it but I, and the Miss Ferrys are **very** anxious that nothing should be said about it."

People talk about the pleasure of antici- pations. I never could see it when I was a child, and **I** don't now. I think it is misery. **That week was the most** uncomfortable week of my life, excepting one which I passed **shut up** in the garret for a punishment, after I had been very naughty. If it had **not** been for lying on the hay-mow with Midge, and talking to her about it, **I** know I should have been sick.

At last the **invitations** came, — all sent

out in one forenoon, two days before Christmas. Such a hubbub as all the children in
town were in! The invitations were written
on bright pink paper.

" The Miss Ferrys request the pleasure of
your company on Christmas Eve, from six
till nine o'clock.

" You will please bring your cat. There
will be a Christmas-tree for the cats.

"Each cat is expected to wear a paper
ruff.

" The servants can be sent to take the cats
home at half-past seven."

I did not know what a ruff was, but
mamma explained it to me, and showed me
the picture of an old queen in one. We
cut one out, and put it on Midge, but she
tore it off in about half a minute; and
mamma said that if the cats were to be
kept in ruffs through the entire evening,
she thought it would be more work than

play; but we could all carry half-a-dozen
extra ones in our pockets, and put them on
occasionally, if Miss Esther and Miss Jane
thought best. I had six for Midge, — one
red, one green, one blue, and three white.
We thought it would be funnier to have a
variety of colors.

By quarter before six o'clock, on Christmas Eve, a droll procession was to be seen
walking towards the yellow cottage. Each
boy and girl carried a cat hugged up
tightly, and as it was pitchy dark, the
cats' eyes shone out like little balls of fire
moving about in the air. We had a dreadful time taking off our things in the hall,
for the cats all began to mew, they were
so frightened. We all wore our everyday
gowns, because our mammas said that the
cats would probably fight, and spill things;
but Miss Esther and Miss Jane were dressed
in their best stiff black silks, and had on

"There sat Tom, and Spunk, and Spitfire, and Yellow,
all in a row."

their biggest gold chains, and we felt quite
ashamed till we forgot about our clothes. I
did not go till six o'clock, for I did not
want to have Midge the first cat in the room,
she was such an ugly little thing; but as
soon as I went into the parlor, I laughed so,
that I dropped her right on the floor, and
she put her paw through her blue ruff, and
tore it off, before Miss Esther had seen it.

There sat Tom, and Spunk, and Spitfire,
and Yellow, all in a row, in their high-chairs,
with enormous paper ruffs on, so big that
ours looked like nothing at all by the side
of them. Tom had a white one; Spitfire
had a deep blue, which was beautiful with
her gray fur; Spunk had a shining black
one; and Yellow's was fiery red. There
they sat as solemn as judges, and everybody
in the room was screaming with laughter.
Six cats beside Midge had already arrived,
and they had all hid under the chairs and

tables, the perfect pictures of misery. Miss
Esther and Miss Jane looked very proud of
their cats, who really did behave as if they
had been all their lives accustomed to re-
ceiving company. "However," I thought to
myself, "it won't last long," and it didn't.
As soon as I saw Willie Dickinson come in
with his old Iron Gray, I knew black Tom
could not keep quiet, for Iron Gray and he
always fought "like cats and dogs." In about
five minutes Tom caught sight of him, and
just as Miss Esther was kissing Bessie White,
who had her tame Maltese kitten tucked
under her arm like a hat, Tom jumped right
over Miss Esther's shoulder, and came down
headforemost between Willie and Bessie, and
stuck his claw into Iron Gray's ear. Willie
sprang to catch up Iron Gray, and trod on
Midge, who began to mew, and for a minute
it looked as if we should have a terrible
time. But Miss Esther snatched Tom up,

and gave him a box on the ears, and put him back into his chair, where he sat looking just as guilty and ashamed as a whipped child; and Willie said he would hold Iron Gray in his lap, so all was soon quiet. As for the rest of the cats, they were as still as mice; two or three of them had crept quite out of sight under the great hair-cloth sofa.

By quarter-past six the company had all arrived: twelve girls, eight boys, and twenty cats. The room was large, but it seemed crowded; and it was quite troublesome to get about without stepping on a cat, especially as everybody was laughing so that they could hardly walk straight.

I soon found out that the only way to feel easy about Midge was to hold her in my arms; but I must say that she behaved as well as any cat there, excepting Lucy Turner's cat Box, which was almost as handsome as Miss Jane's yellow, and had been trained to sit on **Lucy's shoulder.** That was the prettiest sight in the room; for Lucy Turner was the prettiest girl in town, and Box's ruff was made of satin paper, of a brilliant green color, which looked beautiful against her own yellow fur, and Lucy's yellow curls.

At half-past six the doors were thrown open into the little library, and there stood the Tree. It was a thick **fir-tree, and it had** twenty splendid Chinese lanterns **on it, all** in a blaze of light. Then there were twenty-four phials **of cream,** tied on by bright red ribbons; twenty-four **worsted** balls, **scarlet** and white **and yellow; and as** many **as two** hundred **gay-colored** *bonbon* papers, with fringe at the ends.

We all took up **our cats in our arms, and** marched **into the room, and** stood around the tree. Then the cats' high-chairs **were** brought in, and placed two on the right, and

two on the left, of the tree; and Tom, and
Spitfire, and Spunk, and Yellow, were put
into them.

I never would have believed that twenty-
four cats could be so still; they all looked
as grave as if they were watching for rats.

Miss Esther rang a bell, and the maid
brought in twenty-four small tin pans on a
waiter; then Miss Jane told us each to take
a phial of cream off the tree and empty it
into a pan for our cat. This took a long
time, for some of the phials hung quite high,
and none of us dared to put our cat down
for a minute. Such a lapping and spattering
as they made drinking up the cream! It
sounded like rain on window-blinds.

After this, Miss Esther distributed the
bonbon papers by handfuls, and told us to
"let the dear cats eat all they could." Some
of the papers had nice bits of roast veal in
them; some had toasted cheese, and some

had chicken-wings. We did not get on very well with this part of the feeding. We tried to keep the cats in our laps, and feed them out of our fingers; but they were more accustomed to eating on the floor, or on the ground, and they would snatch the meat out of our hands, in spite of all we could do, and jump down with it in their teeth. Then one cat would see another with a bit of meat which looked nicer than her own, and she would drop hers, and fly to quarrelling and snatching after the other. They all wanted chicken-wings; after once tasting of those, they despised the roast veal, and even the cheese, and as there were only a few chicken-wings, it made trouble. Before we got through with this, we were rather tired; and the cats, too, had more than they ought to eat, and began to get fretful, just like children who have been stuffed; there must have been thirty or forty

of the *bonbon* papers left on the tree; but
Miss Esther said they would do for the cats'
breakfasts the next day, so they would not be
wasted. It seemed ungrateful, after the old
ladies had taken so much pains to amuse us,
to find any fault with the party; but we did
begin to feel hungry, and to think that the
cats need not have had everything. At last
I saw Willie Dickinson turn his back to
the people, and slyly bite a mouthful off a
chicken-wing before he gave it to Iron Gray.
This made me hungrier than ever; and I am
ashamed to say, that I, too, watched my
chance, and popped a bit of veal into my
mouth when I thought nobody was looking.
Fancy my mortification when I heard Miss
Esther's kind voice behind me, saying, — "I
am afraid our little friends are getting hungry. Their turn will come by and by."
Oh, I wished the floor would open and swallow me up. I have never been so ashamed

3

since, and I never can be, if I live a hundred years.

All this time, Tom, and Spitfire, and Spunk, and Yellow sat up in their high-chairs as grand as so many kings on thrones, and had two little tables before them, off which they ate. Really they hardly looked like cats, they were so dignified and so large. If they had only known it, though, it was not very civil of them to be sitting up in that way, at their own party, the only ones who had either a chair or a table, but it was not their fault.

At last Miss Esther said, — "Now we will give the cats a game of ball to wind up with," and she took a red worsted ball from the tree, and threw it out into the parlor. Midge sprang after it like lightning; then we all took balls and threw them out, and let all the cats run after them, and for a few minutes there was a fine jumble and tumble of cats and balls on the floor. But as soon as the cats found out that the balls were not something more to eat, all except the very young ones walked off and sat down, just like grown-up men and women, round the sides of the room. This was the funniest sight of all, for they all began to wash their faces and their paws; and to see twenty cats at once doing this is droller than can be imagined. In the middle of the floor lay the bright balls, and Midge and three other kittens were rolling over and over among them. We all laughed till we were so tired we could not speak, and most of us had tears rolling down our cheeks.

Pretty soon the door-bell rang; the maid came into the parlor and said, —

"Judge Dickinson's man has come after Willie's cat."

Then we all laughed harder than ever, and Willie called out, —

"That is no way to speak. You should say, 'Mr. Iron Gray's carriage has come.'"

Next came our Bridget after Midge, and I must say I was glad to get rid of her. In a few minutes the cats were all gone; then we looked at each other and wondered what we should do next. Tom and Spunk had got down from their chairs and gone to sleep before the fire; and Yellow and Spitfire were playing with the bits of paper which were scattered on the floor. What with the *bonbon* papers, and the torn ruffs, it looked like a paper-mill. We were just proposing a game of Blind Man's Buff, when the maid opened the dining-room door, and oh, how we jumped and screamed when we saw the fine supper-table which was set out for us! It was a nice old-fashioned sit-down supper, such as nobody gives nowadays; and the things to eat were all wholesome and plain, so that nobody could be made sick by eating all they chose. Miss Esther and Miss Jane walked around the tables all the time, and slipped apples and oranges into our pockets for us to carry home, and kept begging us to eat more chicken and bread and butter. When we went away, we each had one of the splendid Chinese lanterns given to us; and there was not a single little girl there, who did not think for years and years afterward that it would be the grandest thing in this world to be an old maid like Miss Esther Ferry, and live in a yellow cottage, with one sister and four big cats.

THE LEGEND OF ST. NICHOLAS.

THE tales of good St. Nicholas
　　Are known in every clime;
Told in painting, and in statues,
　　And in the poet's rhyme.
For centuries they've worshipped him,
　　In churches east and west;
Of all the saints we read about
　　He is beloved the best.
Because he was the saint of all
　　The wretched and the poor,
And never sent a little child
　　Uusuccored from his door.
In England's isle, alone, to-day,
　　Four hundred churches stand
Which bear his name, and keep it well
　　Remembered through the land.
And all the little children
　　In England know full well
This tale of good St. Nicholas,
　　Which I am now to tell.

The sweetest tale, I think, of all
  The tales they tell of him;
I never read it but my eyes
  With tears begin to swim.

There was a heathen king who roved
  About with cruel bands,
And waged a fierce and wicked war
  On all the Christian lands.
And once he took as captive
  A little fair-haired boy,
A Christian merchant's only son,
  His mother's pride and joy.
He decked him in apparel gay,
  And said, "You're just the age
To serve behind my chair at meat,
  A dainty Christian page."
Oh, with a sore and aching heart
  The lonely captive child
Roamed through the palace, big and grand,
  And wept and never smiled.
And all the heathen jeered at him,
  And called him Christian dog,
And when the king was angry
  He kicked him like a log,

And spat upon his face, and said:
  "Now by my beard, thy gods
Are poor to leave their worshippers
  At such unequal odds."

One day, just as the cruel king
  Had sat him down to dine,
And in his jewelled cup of gold
  The page was pouring wine,
The little fellow's heart ran o'er
  In tears he could not stay,
For he remembered suddenly,
  It was the very day
On which the yearly feast was kept
  Of good St Nicholas,
And at his home that very hour
  Were dancing on the grass,
With music, and with feasting, all
  The children of the town.
The king looked up, and saw his tears;
  His face began to frown:
"How now, thou dog! thy snivelling tears
  Are running in my cup;
'Twas not with these, but with good wine,
  I bade thee fill it up.

Why weeps the hound?"   The child replied:
  " I weep, because to-day,
In name of good St. Nicholas,
  All Christian children play;
And all my kindred gather home,
  From greatest unto least,
And keep to good St. Nicholas
  A merry banquet feast."
The heathen king laughed scornfully:
  " If he be saint indeed,
Thy famous great St. Nicholas,
  Why does he not take heed
To thee to-day, and bear thee back
  To thy own native land?
Ha! well I wot, he cannot take
  One slave from out my hand!"

Scarce left the boastful words his tongue
  When, with astonished eyes,
The cruel king a giant form
  Saw swooping from the skies.
A whirlwind shook the palace walls,
  The doors flew open wide,
And lo! the good St. Nicholas
  Came in with mighty stride.

Right past the guards, as they were not,
　Close to the king's gold chair,
With striding steps the good Saint came,
　And seizing by his hair
The frightened little page, he bore
　Him, in a twinkling, high
Above the palace topmost roof,
　And vanished in the sky.

Now at that very hour was spread
　A banquet rich and dear,
Within the little page's home,
　To which, from far and near,
The page's mourning parents called
　All poor to come and pray
With them, to good St. Nicholas,
　Upon his sacred day.
Thinking, perhaps, that he would heal
　Their anguish and their pain,
And at poor people's prayers might give
　Their child to them again.

Now what a sight was there to see,
　When flying through the air,
The Saint came carrying the boy,
　Still by his curly hair!

THE LEGEND OF ST. NICHOLAS.

And set him on his mother's knee,
  Too frightened yet to stand,
And holding still the king's gold cup
  Fast in his little hand.
And what glad sounds were these to hear,
  What sobs and joyful cries,
And calls for good St. Nicholas,
  To come back from the skies!
But swift he soared, and only smiled,
  And vanished in the blue;
Most likely he was hurrying
  Some other good to do.
But I wonder if he did not stop
  To take a passing look
Where still the cruel heathen king
  In terror crouched and shook;
While from the palace all his guards
  In coward haste had fled,
And told the people, in his chair
  The king was sitting dead.

Hurrah for good St. Nicholas!
  The friend of all the poor,
Who never sent a little child
  Unsuccored from his door.

We do not pray to saints to-day,
But still we hold them dear,
And the stories of their holy lives
Are stories good to hear.
They are a sort of parable,
And if we ponder well,
We shall not find it hard to read
The lesson which they tell.
We do not pray to saints to-day,
Yet who knows but they hear
Our mention of them, and are glad
We hold their memory dear?
Hurrah for good St. Nicholas,
The friend of all the poor,
Who never sent a little child
Unsuccored from his door!

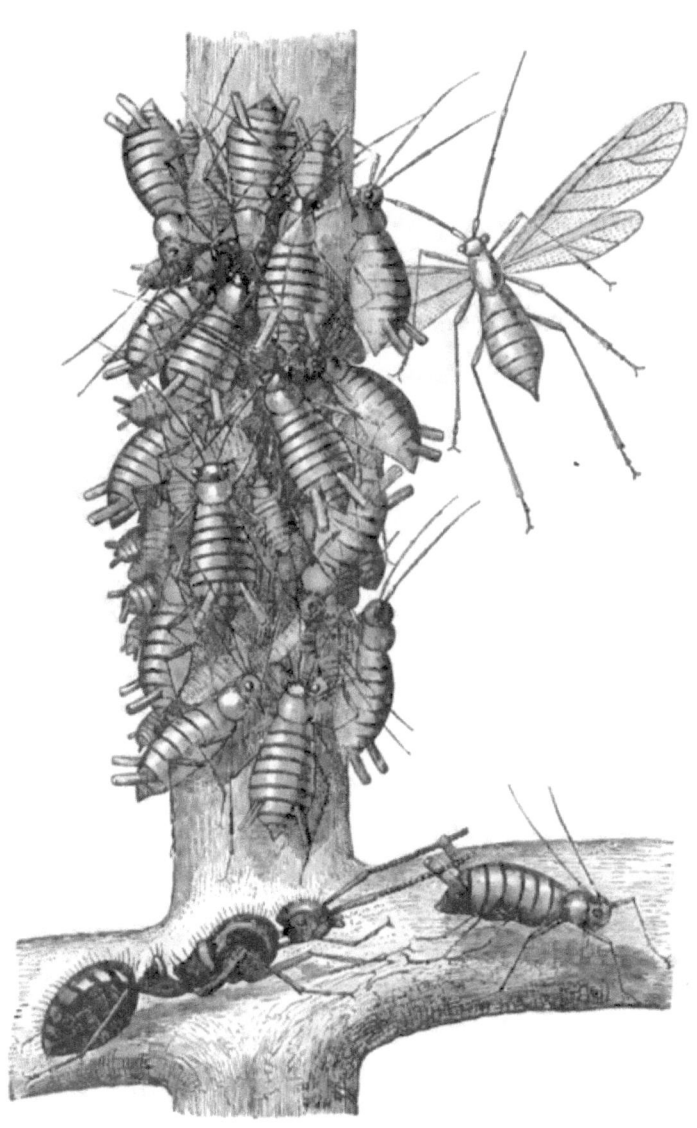

My Ant's Cow.

MY ANT'S COW.

MY Ant lives in the country and keeps a cow. I am ashamed to say that, although I have always known she was a most interesting person, I never went to see her until last week. I am afraid I should not have gone then, if I had not found an account of her, and her house, and her cow, in a book which I was reading.

"Dear me," said I, "and there she has been living so near me all this time, and I never have been to call on her." To tell the truth, it was much worse than that; I had often met her in the street, and had taken such a dislike to her looks that I always brushed by as quickly as possible without speaking to her. But I knew that she had never taken any notice of me, so I hoped she would not recognize me, if I went to call on her, and behaved very politely, now that I had found out how famous she had become. I had great difficulty in finding her house, though it is quite large. She belongs to a very peculiar family; they prefer to live in the dark; so they have no windows in their houses, only doors; and the doors are nothing but holes in the roof. The houses are built in shape of a mound, and not more than ten inches high; they are built out of old bits of wood, dead leaves, straw, old bones; in short, every sort of old thing that they find they stick in the walls of their houses. Their best rooms are all down cellar; and dark enough they must be on a rainy day, when the doors are always kept shut tight.

But I ought to have told you about my Ant herself before I told you about her house; when you hear what an odd person she is, you will not be surprised to know in what an outlandish kind of house she lives. To begin with, I must tell you that she belongs to a most aristocratic family, and never does any work. You'd never suppose so, to see her. I really think she is the queerest-looking creature I ever met. In the first place, her skin is of a dark brown color, darker than an Indian's, and she has six legs. Of course she can walk three times as fast as if she had only two, — but I would rather go slower and be more like other people. She has frightful jaws, with which she does all sorts of things besides eating. She uses them for tweezers, pick-axes, scissors, knife and fork, and in case of a battle, for swords. Then she has growing out of the front part of her head two long slender horns, which she keeps moving about continually in all directions, and with which she touches everything she wishes to understand. The first thing she does, when she meets you, is to bend both these horns straight towards you, and feel of you all over. It is quite disagreeable,—almost as bad as shaking hands with strangers.

My Ant's name is Formica Rufa. If I knew her better I should call her Ant Ru, for short. But I do not expect ever to know her very well; she evidently does not like to be intimate with anybody but her own family; and I don't so much wonder, for I never was in any house so overrun with people as hers is. I wondered how they knew themselves apart. When I went to see her last week I found her just going out, and I thought perhaps that was one reason she didn't take any more notice of me.

"How do you do, Ant?" said I. "I am spending the summer near by, and thought I would like to become acquainted with you.

I hear you have a very curious cow, and I have a great desire to see it."

"Humph!" said she, and snapped her horns up and down, as she always does when she is displeased, I find.

Then I realized that it was a mistake to mention in the first place that I had come to see the cow. But it was too late to take it back. That is the worst of these awkward truths that sometimes slip out in spite of us; there is no putting them out of sight again.

However, I went on, trying to conciliate her as well as I could, in my entire ignorance of the rules of behavior in the society to which she belonged.

"I hope it will not give you any trouble to show her to me. You must be very proud of having such a fine cow. Perhaps you are on the way to milking now, and if so I should be most happy to go with you."

"Humph!" said my Ant again. At least I

4

think that was what she said. It looked
like it. I can't say that I heard any distinct
articulate sound; and I was too embarrassed
to listen very attentively, for I did begin to
feel that she might resent my coming out of
mere curiosity to see her cow, when I had
lived to be an old woman without ever going
near her.

But she turned short on her heels (I
suppose she has heels), and plunged into
the woods at the right, stopping and looking
back at me as if she expected me to follow.
So I stepped along after her as fast as I
could, and said, "Thank you; I suppose this
is the way to the pasture."

My Ant said nothing, but went ahead,
snapping her horns furiously.

"Oh, well," thought I to myself, "you're
an uncivil Ant anyhow, if I have come simply
out of curiosity. You might be a little
more polite in your own house, or at least

on your own grounds, which is the same thing. I sha'n't speak to you again," and that's about all the conversation I have ever had with my Ant. But she took me to the pasture, and I saw her cow.

I am almost afraid to tell you where the pasture was, and what the cow was; but if you don't believe me, you can look in books written about such things, and they will convince you that every word I say is true. The pasture was the stalk of a green brier; and there stood not only my Ant's cow, but as many as five hundred others, all feeding away upon it. You have seen millions of them in your lives; I dare say have killed them by teaspoonfuls; for you must know that they were nothing but little green lice, such as sometimes kill our rose-bushes, and we try in every possible way to get rid of. Who would ever suppose there could be a race of creatures for whom these

little green plant-lice could serve as cows!
But I assure you it is true, and if you live
in the country you can see **it for yourself**;
but you will have to look through a magnifying-glass **to see** them milked.   Think of
looking through a magnifying-glass at anybody's cow! I looked at **my** Ant's for an
hour, **and it** seemed to mé I hardly winked,
I was so absorbed in the curious sight.

Its skin **was** smooth as satin **and of a**
most beautiful light green color.   It had six
legs, and little hooks at the end, instead of
hoofs; the oddest thing of all was that the
horns **were not on its head,** but at the other
end of **its body, where the tail** would have
been, if **it had** had a **tail like** any other **cow;**
the horns are hollow tubes, and it is out of
them that the milk comes, a drop at a time.
The milk is meant for the little plant-lice to
suck before they are old enough **to hook**
their six legs on **to stalks** and leaves, and

feed on sap. But I think that in any place where there are many of my Ant's race, the little plant-lice must fare as badly as poor little calves do when men shut them up away from their mothers; for the Ants are so fond of this milk that sometimes they carry off whole herds of the plant-lice and shut them up in chambers in their houses, and feed them as we do cows in barns, and go and milk them whenever they please.

"Oh, dear Ant," said I to my Ant, "do pray milk your cow! I have such a desire to see how you do it."

She did not appear to understand me, and I dare say if she had she would not have done it any sooner. But presently I saw her go up behind her cow, and begin to tap her gently on her back, just at the place where the horns grew out. The cow did not look round nor stop eating, but in a moment out came a tiny drop of liquid from

the tip of each tube; my Ant picked it up
with her wonderful horns and whisked it
into her mouth as quick as you would a
sugar-plum.   Then she went on to the next
cow and milked that in the same manner,
and then a third one; she took only two
drops from each one.   Perhaps that is all
that this kind of cow can give at a time.
However, I think that for my Ant to take
that one drop at a mouthful was about the
same in proportion to her size that it would
be for us to take a gallon at a swallow.   So
after all, by milking her own cow and two of
her neighbors', she made quite a respectable
meal.   There were several of her friends
there at the same time doing their milking;
and I could not help thinking how easy it
would be for the great herd of cows to kill
my Ant and all her race, if they chose.
But it is thought by wise people who have
studied these wonderful things that the cows

are fond of being milked in this way, and would be sorry to be left alone by themselves.

After my Ant had finished her supper, she stood still watching the cows for some time. I thought perhaps she would be in a better humor after having had so much to eat, and might possibly feel like talking with me. But I was determined not to speak first. So I sat still and tried to look as if I did not care whether she spoke or not, for I have observed that that is the surest way to make sullen and contrary people talk. But she never once opened her mouth, though I think I sat there a good hour and a half. At last it began to grow dark, and as I had quite a long walk to take, I knew I must go, or I should not get home in time for my own supper of milk.

"Good-night, Ant," said I. "I have had a charming visit. I am very much obliged to you indeed for showing me your cow. I think she is the most wonderful creature I ever saw. I should be very happy to see you at my house."

"Humph!" said my Aunt.

ST. MARTIN'S CLOAK.

ST. MARTIN was a soldier
    Of Constantine the Great;
While yet he was a stripling
    He bore full armor's weight;
He fought right well and valiantly;
    No worse because he prayed;
His comrades sometime scoffed at him,
    When the cross's sign he made.
But they loved him in their hearts,
    And revered his saintly life,
And felt safer with him close to them,
    In the thickest of the strife.

They tell a many tales of him;
    His generosity;
His love for all the poor; his deeds
    Of gracious charity;
Above them all, this one is sweet
    And wonderful to read,
And holds a tender lesson
    For us to learn and heed.

Oh if we lived to-day, as lived
    Those blessed ancient saints,
This world of ours less full would be
    Of weeping and complaints.

One dreadful winter, when the cold
    Was so bitter that it killed
Men on the streets, and, spite of fires,
    In houses they were chilled,
St. Martin went one morning
    To pass the city's gate,
And there he saw a ragged man,
    Whose pitiable state
So moved his heart, that in a trice
    He drew his good broadsword,
And cut his warm fur cloak in two
    Without a single word,
And threw the beggar-man one-half;
    Then in the other, clad
But meagrely, he rode all day .
    Half frozen, but most glad.

At night, St. Martin dreamed a dream,
    Such dreams as angels bring;
They led him in his dream to Heaven,
    To see a wondrous thing.

He saw the Good Lord walking
  Along the golden street,
With angels crowding round him,
  On silver pinions fleet;
And lo, upon his shoulders
  A wrap of fur he bore,
The self-same wrap of fur which matched
  The half St. Martin wore!

And turning to the angels,
  With smile, the Good Lord said,
"Now do ye know, my angels,
  Who thus hath me array'd?
My servant Martin hath done this,
  Though he is unbaptized,
And dreameth not his charity
  By me is known and prized."

The next day, while the vision
  Glowed within him like a flame,
Young Martin sought a holy priest,
  Who baptized him in God's name.
And after that, for thirty years
  He fought the Emperor's fights
As one whose eye and hand are nerved
  By Heaven's sounds and sights.

RUNNA RIG.

THE NAUGHTY FAIRY WHO PLAYED WITH FIRE.

ONE cold night in March, when the wind blew wildly and shook the windows, I sat alone in a small garret-room, which was lit only by one candle. The candle had burned nearly out; not more than two inches of it was left, and that did not stand very firmly in the candlestick. The room was cold and seemed quite dark. I was thinking of some one whom I loved so much, that while I thought the tears came into my eyes. It is very strange, but when our eyes are full of tears of love, we can see more clearly than at any other time. Sometimes I think that if we always looked through such tears

we could see into Heaven, but this night I
only got a peep into Fairy Land.

As I looked steadily at the flame of the
candle, I suddenly observed, for the first
time in my life, how tall and stiff the round
black wick stood up in the middle of it.
The flame was nearly an inch high, shaped
like an arched gate, blue, and looked almost
solid at bottom, pale yellow, and quite trans-
parent at top; the slender black thread of
the burning wick came half-way to the top
of the arch, and stood firm as a little ebony
soldier, while the blaze swayed about it. I
blew the flame gently, and then harder, but
the small black figure did not stir. As I
looked at it more carefully, I saw that it had
a head. The longer I looked, the darker
the room grew, and at last I lost sight of
the candlestick, table, everything except the
arch of fire, with a patient, erect little figure
in the centre of it, looking directly at me

out of two bright red eyes. I thought it was very odd that I had never noticed before how much the wicks of candles looked like tiny black boys. While I was wondering if they always looked so, the figure tottered, and I took up the snuffers to snuff the candle.

Think how I jumped, when out of the little bit of a black head came a little bit of a voice, crying:

"Oh! don't cut me off! don't cut me off!"

Of course I knew at once that it must be a fairy, but I thought to myself, I won't be afraid while he speaks English; so I said:

"No, indeed, you funny little manikin, I won't cut you off; however, if I don't, you'll tumble down in a minute into this boiling fat, and that will be worse than to be jammed in the hinges of the snuffers. But how did you ever get into the candlewick, and don't you very much dislike being there?"

"Oh, dear! I think I do," said he; "but unless you can contrive to prop me up, I shall not have time to tell you anything, and I would like to tell you who I am and how I came here."

I propped the wick up as well as I could with the snuffers and two sticks, so that I thought it would last long enough for such a mite of a fairy to tell all he knew, and then I begged him to use short words, and skip all about the time when he was a baby, and perhaps he could get through. His voice was a droll little voice, finer than the finest squeak you ever heard from a kitten. I had to listen with all my might to understand what he said, and in spite of all my pains, I now and then lost a word. It was queer that such a little thread of a voice could sound like crying, but it really did, and the melting wax of the candle bubbled round his feet, too, which made it all the harder to hear him. I shall tell his story to you in his own words, for they are much better than mine would be : —

The Fairy's Story.

"My name is Runna Rig, and that in fairy language means mischief. I have always thought that if I had only been called by some other name, I should never have got into any trouble, for my brother Taik Tyme and my sister Nevva Dew Raung have always lived peaceably and in comfort, but I have never done anything but mischief since I was born, and I have had more punishments than I could tell you. This one I am bearing now, however, is so much worse than any of the others, that they all look like play to me as I remember them.

When I tell you the cause of this one,
you will not think it too severe. I myself own that it is just. If I had been in
the Queen's place, I would have made it
harder still; though I am sure I don't know
what could be harder," groaned the poor
little fellow. "Do you suppose you have
the slightest idea how hot it is in here? But
I must make haste and tell you what it was
that I did.

"One day, as my brother and I were
taking a nap on a burdock-leaf, we were
waked up by a loud noise. We ran in great
fright to the top of the tallest stem of the
burdock, and there we saw at a little dis-
tance two human children, with small pine-
sticks in their hands, tipped with something
bright yellow, which shone in the sun.
These sticks they struck with great force
against a rock, and immediately there followed a tremendous noise, and a great fire

5

which lit up the whole place, **while the blazing** bits **of yellow** stone **fell** on **all** sides. **My** brother **was too frightened to** speak, **but I thought** it **the most beautiful** sight **I** had ever seen, and **I longed to have** a piece of the yellow stone myself, **and see** what I could do with it. **After the children** went away, **we** crept down, **and found the** ground covered with **small** sparkling **pieces** of the precious yellow. **I begged Taik Tyme** to help **me carry some of it home.** At first he would not have anything **to do** with it, but finally consented, **more to please** me than because he cared for **it himself.** It is **wonderful to** see any being with so little curiosity as **my** brother has. **We collected** a great quantity **of it, as much as we could** pile on a large plantain-leaf, **which we lifted** carefully by the edges and carried **home.** Just as **we** reached the edge **of** Periwinkle Path, in which **we** lived, the **weight of** the

yellow stone split the leaf, and it all fell
through to the ground, which gave us a
great deal of trouble. At last we got it
safely hid under a bed of old red poppy-
leaves, where some strolling beggars had
slept the night before, and near which we
knew that no one would go. By this time
my brother had been made so ill by the
smell of the strange stuff, that he could not
eat any supper; which was a dreadful pity,
for we had some rare mignonette honey,
which had been sent by my uncle, who is
High Steward to the Queen.

"I could not sleep all night for thinking
of my treasures, and planning how I should
make my experiments. It was a stormy
night, the wind blew like a hurricane, and
rocked the whole garden. Some neighbors
of ours, who had known no better than to
go to sleep in the upper story of a honey-
suckle, were blown out of their beds just

before morning. I was thankful that I had thought to put some large stones on the edges of the poppy-leaves to hold them down; afterward, I wished that I had not done any such thing, and that they had all blown away, yellow stones and all, in the night.

"I was up before light, and ran to the poppy-bed. All was safe. But now I could not think of any way to fasten the yellow stone to the ends of sticks, and I did not dare to fire them off in any other way. In despair, I called my bosom friend Karefanaut, showed him my treasures, and told him what I had seen the children do.

"'Oh! I know all about that,' said he. 'It is something which comes on the end of what they call matches. I have often seen children playing with them. It is perfectly splendid. How did you get it? But, bah!

what an odor ! It must be that human beings
have no sense of smell ! '

"Finally, Karefanaut proposed that we
should put a piece of it on a flat stone, and
then let another stone fall on it from a great
height; that, he thought, would make it
explode. It was not easy to do this, but it
worked capitally. We lugged heavy stones,
almost as large as ourselves, up to the tops
of bushes, and threw them down on the
piece of yellow stone which we had arranged
below. 'Bang!' 'Pop!' off it went, and
sometimes a very little blaze and smoke
came with it. But the best part of all was
to see everybody run. Everybody thought
it came from the sky, and everybody began
to think that the world must be coming to
an end. For weeks, Karefanaut and I spent
all our time in this way. Nobody suspected
us; in fact, the noises and smells were so
very queer that nobody could help believing

that something dreadful must be going on in the world, of which we knew nothing. The two wisest men of the court, Digg Phoreva and Peer Abaut, wrote treatises to prove that the earth was getting too close to the sun, and that we should all be burnt up in six years. The Queen called a solemn, secret council under the White Rose, to decide whether we had not better all take refuge with her brother, the King of the Wood-mice. Nobody talked of anything except these terrible sounds and smells, and Karefanaut and I were ready to die a-laughing from morning till night. How little we dreamed of the misery in store for us !

"You may not think so, seeing me now," continued the fairy, leaning sadly against the snuffers, and bowing his little head under the arch of flame ; "but, really, Karefanaut and I had a merry time of it as long as the yellow stone held out. At last, we had used it all up except one large piece, which was so heavy we could not move it. This was a piece which Karefanaut had found under the burdock; he had harnessed two beetles to it, and drawn it home in the night. It was quite a rock, and we knew would make a grand explosion.

"Finally, Karefanaut, who had a reputation as a student of science, gave out that he was going to try some experiments in distilling the juice of poppies, of which a great deal was used in the Queen's nurseries as soothing-syrup. So we built a tower in the poppy-bed over our precious rock, and carried up into the top of it many heavy stones. The tower was so built that by pulling out one board at the bottom, the whole would fall. To this board we fastened a strong chain, the end of which we carried just under ground, a long way outside of the garden. We knew better than to be very near when this explosion took place. For some weeks, after all was ready, we delayed. Karefanaut, for the first time in his life, was afraid, and I could do nothing without him, as it took all the strength of both to lift the chain. At last, he grew ashamed of his fears, and hurried me off one morning before I had finished my breakfast.

"The Queen was giving a grand entertainment in honor of the marriage of her youngest daughter, Fli Fasta, to her cousin, Heavi Stepp, from the seashore, and we thought that, perhaps, the noise would not be noticed so much when the court was all agog about this. Alas! what a mistake!

"It was a long time before we could start the chain, — it seemed to have rusted in the ground. At last it gave way so suddenly that Karefanaut and I both fell over backward, and hurt ourselves severely. Between

the pain of the fall and the frightful noise
which followed when the tower fell, we were
too frightened to stir, and lay on the ground
for an hour, looking at each other without
speaking a word. Then I said :

"'We may as well go home first as last,
I suppose.'

"'No,' said Karefanaut, 'I think not; the
longer we are away, the less likely we shall
be to be suspected. They will think that
the tower blew up of itself; and we can say
that we have been over in the fir-wood,
hunting.'

"This seemed to me very good advice; so
I bound up an ugly cut on my head with
clover-blossoms, and went to sleep on a tuft
of grass. I slept all day, for I was utterly
tired out. When I waked, Karefanaut had
gone. I did not know what to make of
this; but I loved him too well to suspect
him of anything wrong.

" I walked slowly toward home, growing more and more unhappy and afraid at every step. Alas! my worst forebodings were nothing. As soon as I reached the border of the garden, I was seized by two of the Queen's archers, who forbade me to speak, and dragged me to prison. The next morning I was taken before the Queen and all the court, and learned that the cowardly and faithless Karefanaut had hastened back before me, to throw himself on their mercy and confess all. He had sworn that I was the contriver of the whole plot, and that I had forced him to help me by the most dreadful threats. I scorned to accuse him in turn, and received my sentence in silence. When I heard of all the frightful ruin which the explosion had caused, I was only too thankful to get off with my life.

" The tower fell at noon, just as the court, after a late breakfast, had dispersed for the

amusements of the day. The young Prince
Heavi Stepp was swinging in the Grand
Fandango, which the Queen had created in
honor of his marriage. It was the most
magnificent one ever seen in our court.
The seats were made of white tiger-lilies,
and would hold eight persons. The ropes
were twisted of the shining threads spun by
black spiders, and there were five thousand
strands to a rope. At the moment of the
explosion, Prince Heavi Stepp had just
asked the Princess Fli Fasta to take her
seat in it with him; but she was afraid, and
he had sprung in alone, to show her that
there was no danger. At that instant the
tower fell. The shock broke six of the
largest ropes, and threw the prince to the
ground. He was not killed, but his nose
and his right leg were broken, so that he
was lamed and disfigured for life. The
princess fainted from fright, and for many

days the doctors thought she would die. The Queen herself did not escape. She was standing under a pink althea canopy, which had been newly put up for her pavilion, when a piece of the blazing stone fell through the top, utterly ruining the pink silk and setting fire to the Queen's dress. A carpenter rolled her up in some blankets of mullein which happened to be lying there, and this was all that saved her life. There were more than twenty gold buttercup-boats sailing in the basin of the fountain, filled with the most beautiful ladies of the court. These were all upset, and three of the maids of honor were drowned. But the saddest thing of all was the burning up of Moss Pink Square. A blazing brand fell right in the middle of it, and the houses were so light and dry, and close together, that they burnt like tinder. All the poor working-people lived there, and they lost nearly everything.

Orl Twisthup, the court tailor, in trying to save the Prince Heavi Stepp's wedding-coat, which was in a closet in his shop, was so badly burned, that he will never be able to sew again. Poor little Utta Trimkin, dress-maker to the Queen, lost all the rare and beautiful cloths which she had bought to make up for the wedding; and some of them could not be replaced, because they were bought of the glass-pedler, who deals with the mermaids, and only comes once in a hundred years. This was the thing I felt worst of all about, for I knew Utta Trim-kin very well, and she was a dear little thing. I felt very sadly, too, about the Princess Fli Fasta's favorite brown caterpillar. She had just ridden him up to the Fandango, and fastened him to a plantain-leaf. He was the only creature in all the Queen's stables that the Princess Fli Fasta dared to mount. Whether he was hit by a piece of the burning stone, or died of fright, could not be told; but he rolled over in a ball, and they found him stiff and dead.

"Now, you will not think our gracious Queen was too severe in condemning me to punishment by fire. I have not told you one-half of the misery and distress which my thoughtless act caused in her kingdom. My punishment will have come to an end long before their traces have disappeared.

"As soon as night comes, I am obliged to take my place in a candlewick, and to stand straight and still till the wick is so burned that it falls of its own accord. If the wick is snuffed, I have to begin again, and this makes it almost more than I can bear. For this reason, I have learned to look for candles ·in garret-rooms like this, where poor people live, for they very seldom snuff their candles.

"My sentence said that I must do this for

two hundred years, — that is, about twenty
years of your time. Only one hundred and
fifty years have gone; but I have great
hopes of being pardoned soon. The Queen
is said to be much pleased with my patience,
and a petition has been sent to her for my
pardon. It cut me to the heart to hear that
Orl Twisthup and Utta Trimkin had both
signed it.

"As for Karefanaut, he has led a miserable life. Everybody despises him, and I
would much rather be in my place than in
his.

"There is one thing which I have the
greatest curiosity to know, which, perhaps,
you can tell me, and that is what sort of
punishment human beings have when they
play with ma ——"

Phiz! sputter! over went the snuffers and
the sticks, — down tumbled the wick. I
jumped up with such a start that I knocked

the candlestick to the floor, and was left in the dark; and that is the end of the fairy Runna Rig's story.

Moral: **Never snuff candles, and** don't play with **fire.**

THE PALACE OF GONDOFORUS.

A LEGEND OF ST. THOMAS.

WHEN King Gondoforus desired
  To have a palace built that should
Be finer than all palaces
  Which in the Roman Empire stood,

He sent his provost Abanes
  To search the countries far and wide
For builders and for architects,
  Whose skill and knowledge had been tried.

Then God unto St. Thomas said:
  " Go, Thomas, now, and tell this king
That thou wilt build a palace which
  Immortal fame to him shall bring."

Then to the saint, Gondoforus
  Gave stores of silver and of gold,
And precious stones and jewels rich;
  Nought did the eager king withhold.

6

" Now see thou build, O saint," he cried,
    All proud and arrogant of mien —
" Now see thou build right speedily
    Such palace as was never seen!"

Then to far countries journeyed he —
    Two years and more he staid away;
At other sovereigns' palaces
    All scornful gazing, he would say:

" St. Thomas, sent from God, doth build
    For me a palace.   God hath said
Its splendor an immortal fame
    Upon my name and reign shall shed."

Gondoforus returned and sought
    With eager haste his palace site;
The field was bare as when he went,
    The sod with peaceful daisies white!

" What has the man called Thomas done
    With all my gold?" he hotly cried.
" Given it all unto the poor,"
    The courtiers sneeringly replied.

The king, in rage no words could tell,
   St. Thomas into prison threw,
And racked his brains to think what he
   For fitting punishment could do.

That very day, his brother died;
   His vengeance now must cool and wait;
Until a royal tomb was built,
   The royal corpse must lie in state.

Lo! on the fourth day sat erect
   The royal corpse, and cried aloud,
While all the mourners and the guards
   Fled terror-stricken in a crowd;

" O king! O brother! listen now,
   These four days I in Paradise
Have wander'd, and return to tell
   Thee what I saw with my own eyes.

" This man whom thou wouldst torture is
   God's servant, dear to God's own heart.
Behold, the angels showed to me
   A palace wrought with wondrous art,

" Of silver, gold, and precious stones:
　　Most marvellously it did shine;
　And when I asked whose **name it bore,**
　　O brother! then they **told me thine!**

" ' St. Thomas this hath **built,'** they said,
　' For **one** Gondoforus, a king.'
　' It is my **brother!'** I exclaimed,
　　And fled to thee the news **to bring."**

　Then **fell the royal corpse again**
　　Back, **silent, solemn in its state;**
　Until the royal **tomb was** built,
　　The royal corpse must lie and wait.

　Oh! **swift** the king the prison **doors,**
　　With his own hands, did open **wide.**
" Come **forth! come forth!** O worthy saint!"
　　He, kneeling on the threshold, cried.

" The dead from heaven this **day hath come,**
　　To tell me how in Paradise
　The palace thou hast built for me
　　Shines beautiful **in angels' eyes.**

" Come forth! come forth! O noble saint!
　And graciously forgive my sin.
As honored guest, my palace gates
　Oh condescend to enter in!"

Then, smiling, said St. Thomas, calm
　And gracious as an angel might:
" O king! didst thou not know that we
　Build not God's palaces in sight

" Of men, nor from the things of earth?
　All heaven lieth full and fair
With palaces which charity
　Alone can build, alone can share.

" Before the world began, were laid
　Their bright foundations by God's hand,
For Charity to build upon,
　As God and his son Christ had planned.

" No other palaces endure;
　No other riches can remain;
No other kingdoms are secure;
　No other kings eternal reign."

Henceforth the king, Gondoforus,
   Went on his way, triumphant, glad,
Remembering what a palace he
   Already in the heavens had.

No more the Roman emperors
   With envy could his bosom move.
How poor their palaces by side
   Of one not made with hands, above!

His treasures in the good saint's hands
   He poured, and left for him to use,
In adding to that palace fair
   Such courts and towers as he might choose.

And there to-day they dwell, I ween,
   With other saints and other kings;
And roam with hosts of angels bright,
   From place to place, on shining wings.

THE ANTS' MONDAY DINNER.

HOW did I know what the ants had for dinner last Monday? Ha, it is odd that I should have known, but I'll tell you how it happened.

I was sitting under a big pine-tree, high up on a high hill-side. The hill-side was more than seven thousand feet above the sea, and that is higher than many mountains which people travel hundreds of miles to look at. But this hill-side was in Colorado, so there was nothing wonderful in being so high up. I had been watching the great mountains with snow on them, and the great forests of pine-trees — miles and miles of them — so close together that it looks as if you could lie down on their tops and not fall through; and my eyes were tired with looking at such great, grand things, so many miles off; so I looked down on the ground where I was sitting, and watched the ants which were running about everywhere, as busy and restless as if they had the whole world on their shoulders.

Suddenly I saw, under a tuft of grass, a tiny yellow caterpillar, which seemed to be bounding along in a very strange way. In a second more, I saw an ant seize hold of him and begin to drag him off. The caterpillar was three times as long as the ant, and his body was more than twice as large round as the biggest part of the ant's body.

"Ho! ho! Mr. Ant," said I, "you needn't think you're going to be strong enough to drag that fellow very far."

Why, it was about the same thing as if you or I should drag off a heifer, which was kicking and struggling for dear life all the time; only that the heifer hasn't half so many legs

to catch hold of things with as the caterpillar had. Poor caterpillar! how he did
try to get away! But the ant never gave
him a second's time to take a good grip of
anything; and he was cunning enough, too,
to drag him on his side, so that he couldn't
use his legs very well. Up and down, and
under and over stones and sticks; in and
out of tufts of grass; up to the very top of
the tallest blades, and then down again;
over gravel and sand, and across bridges of
pine-needles from stone to stone; backward
all the way — but for all I could see, just
as swiftly as if he were going headforemost
—ran that ant, dragging the caterpillar
after him. I watched him very closely,
thinking, of course, he must be making for
his house. Presently, he darted up the
trunk of the pine-tree.

"Dear me!" said I, "ants don't live in
trees! What does this mean?"

The bark of the tree was all broken and jagged, and full of seams twenty times as deep as the height of the ant's body. But he didn't mind; down one side and up the other he went. They must have been awful chasms to him; and to the poor caterpillar too, for their sharp edges caught and tore his skin, and doubled him up a dozen ways in a minute. And yet the ant never once stopped or went a bit slower. I had to watch very closely, not to lose sight of him altogether. I began to think that he was merely trying to kill the caterpillar; that, perhaps, he didn't mean to eat him, after all. Perhaps he was merely a gentlemanly sportsman ant, out on a frolic. How did I know but some ants might hunt caterpillars, just as some men hunt deer, for fun, and not at all because they need food? If I had been sure of this, I would have spoiled Mr. Ant's sport for him very soon, you may be sure,

and set the poor caterpillar free. But I
never heard of an ant's being cruel; and if
it were really for dinner for his family that
he was working so hard, I thought he ought
to be helped, and not hindered. Just then
my attention was diverted from him by a
sharp cry overhead. I looked up, and there
was an enormous hawk, sailing round in
circles, with two small birds flying after
him, pouncing down on his head, and then
darting away, and all the time making shrill
cries of fright and hatred. I knew very
well what that meant. Mr. Hawk was also
out trying to do some marketing for his
dinner; and he had his eye on some little
birds in their nest; and there were the
father and mother birds driving him away.
You wouldn't have believed two such little
birds could have driven off such a big creature as the hawk, but they did. They
seemed to fairly buzz round his head as flies

do round a horse's head, and at last he just gave up and flew off so far that he vanished in the blue sky, and the little birds came skimming home again into the wood.

"Well, well," said I, " the little people are stronger than the big ones, after all! Where has my ant gone?"

Sure enough! It hadn't been two minutes that I had been watching the hawk and the birds, but in that two minutes the ant and the caterpillar had disappeared. At last I found them, — where do you think? In a fold of my water-proof cloak, on which I was sitting! The ant had let go of the caterpillar, and was running round and round him, perfectly bewildered; and the caterpillar was too near dead to stir. I shook the fold out, and as soon as the cloth lay straight and smooth, the ant fastened his nippers in the caterpillar again, and started

off as fast as ever. I suppose if I could
have seen his face, and had understood the
language of ants' features, I should have
seen plainly written there, "Dear me, what
sort of a country was that I tumbled into,
so frightfully black and smooth?" By this
time the caterpillar had had the breath pretty
well knocked out of his body, and was so
limp and helpless that the ant was not afraid
of his getting away from him. So he stopped
a second now and then to rest. Sometimes
he would spring on the caterpillar's back,
and stretch himself out there; sometimes he
would stand still on one side and look at
him sharply, keeping one nipper on his head.
All the time, though, he was working steadily
in one direction; he was headed for home
now, I felt very certain. It astonished me
very much at first, that none of the ants he
met took any notice of him; they all went
on their own way, and never took so much

as a sniff at the caterpillar. But pretty soon I said to myself,—

"You stupid woman, not to suppose that ants can be as well behaved as people! When you passed Mr. Jones yesterday, you didn't peep into his market-basket, nor touch the big cabbage he had under his arm."

Presently, the ant dropped the caterpillar, and ran on a few steps — I mean inches — to meet another ant who was coming towards him. They put their heads close together for a second. I could not hear what they said, but I could easily imagine, for they both ran quickly back to the caterpillar, and one took him by the head and the other by the tail, and then they lugged him along finely. It was only a few steps, however, to the ant's house; that was the reason he happened to meet this friend just coming out. The door was a round hole in the ground, about as big as my little finger.

Several ants were standing in the door-way, watching these two come up with the caterpillar. They all took hold as soon as the caterpillar was on the door-step, and almost before I knew he was fairly there, they had tumbled him down, heels over head, into the ground, and that was the last I saw of him.

The oddest thing was, how the ants came running home from all directions. I don't believe there was any dinner-bell rung, though there might have been one too fine for my ears to hear; but in less than a minute, I had counted thirty-three ants running down that hole. I fancied they looked as hungry as wolves.

I had a great mind to dig down into the hole with a stick, and see what had become of the caterpillar. But I thought it wasn't quite fair to take the roof off a man's house to find out how he cooks his beef for dinner;

so I sat still awhile, and wondered whether they would lay him out straight on the floor, and all stand in rows each side of him and nibble across, and whether they would leave any for Tuesday : and then I went home to my own dinner.

THE NEST.

UNDER the apple-tree, somebody said,
  Look at that robin's nest overhead!
All of sharp sticks, and of mud and clay —
What a rough home for a summer day!"
Gaunt stood the apple-tree, gaunt and bare,
And creaked in the winds which blustered there.
The nest was wet with the April rain;
The clay ran down in an ugly stain;
Little it looked, I must truly say,
Like a lovely home for a summer day.

Up in the apple-tree, somebody laughed,
"Little you know of the true home-craft.
  Laugh if you like, at my sticks and clay;
  They'll make a good home for a summer day.
May turns the apple-tree pink and white,
Sunny all day, and fragrant all night.
My babies will never feel the showers,
For rain can't get through these feathers of ours.
Snug under my wings they will cuddle and creep,
The happiest babies awake or asleep,"
Said the robin-mother, flying away
After more of the sticks and mud and clay.

7

Under the apple-tree somebody sighed,
"Ah me, the blunder of folly and pride!
  The roughest small house of mud or clay
  Might be a sweet home for a summer day,
  Sunny and fragrant all day, all night,
  With only good cheer for fragrance and light;
  And the bitterest storms of grief and pain
  Will beat and break on that home in vain,
  Where a true-hearted mother broods alway,
  And makes the whole year like a summer day."

THE FESTIVAL OF SAN EUSTACHIO IN ROME.

THE little children in Rome do not get their holiday-presents on Christmas; they have them almost two weeks later, on the sixth of January. This is because the Roman Catholics think that was the day on which the wise men brought their gifts to the babe Christ Jesus, in the stable in Bethlehem. And they do not say, as the Germans do, that the dear little Christ-child brings the presents; or, as we do, that jolly Santa Claus comes riding round in the air, above the chimney-tops, and drops the presents down. They tell quite a gloomy story about an old woman they call the Bifana. They say that when the wise men went by her house, carrying the presents

to the baby Jesus, somebody called to her
to come to the window and see them; but
she said she was too busy to stop, she would
see them when they came back. But the
wise men, you know, went out of Judea by
another road; and the story says, that to
this day the old woman is watching, watching for the wise men to come back; and as
often as Twelfth Night comes round she has
to fly over the earth, carrying the presents
to the children. To the good children she
gives nice things; but to the bad ones, only
bags of ashes. I always felt very sorry for
the poor little Roman children, to think
that they did not hear about the beautiful
Christ-kindchen, or our good St. Nicholas.
However, they have a very good time out of
their "Ekifania," which is the name they
give the festival; and I will tell you about
the place where most of the presents are
sold.

It is in the square of San Eustachio, which is almost in the middle of Rome, and very near the Pantheon.

For three hundred and fifty-five days in the year this square, or " piazza," as it is called in Italian, is quite dull and dingy-looking, and has only a few common shops and little booths on the side of the street, where common wares are sold. But for ten days before Twelfth Night, it is so full of booths, and stalls, and shelves, and piles of things to be sold, that one cannot drive through it. Here come all the Roman fathers and mothers who are not very rich; they bring their children and buy presents for them.

The rich people go to fine shops on the Corso, which is the Broadway of Rome, and buy much handsomer things; but I do not believe their children have half such fun as the little children do who can go into the square of San Eustachio at night.

One winter I went myself, with a Roman girl, whose name was Marianina. She was our servant, and she was seventeen years old, and she went to take care of me; but I felt all the time as if I had a child with me who was about nine. She enjoyed it so much, and laughed so hard all the time, that I liked it much better being alone with her, and trying to make believe that I was another Roman girl, than I should to have gone with people of my own race.

It was a bitter cold night. The **Tra Montana** (that is the Roman name for the wind that comes down from the **mountains**) blew furiously; but Marianina had nothing on her head, only a little shawl over her shoulders, and no gloves on her hands. She never had anything on her head in her life, unless, perhaps, a white pocket-handkerchief; all the **poor** women in Rome go bareheaded.

Our house was in the Via Quattro Fontane.

Is not that a pretty name? It means the street of the Four Fountains; and there really were four fountains in it. Up at top of the hill, above our house, where another street crossed, a fountain was set in each corner, with a great dusty old stone statue lying behind it, that looked as if it had lain there for hundreds of years. The hill was so steep that I never liked to see horses drawing a carriage up it; almost every day some poor horse tumbled down on his knees trying to get up. The streets in Rome are all paved with little bits of lava, which are very slippery. So I said to Marianina on this night: "We will walk down to the Barberini Piazza, and get into a little carriage there; I will not have a horse come up this steep hill to-night."

The Barberini Piazza was a square at the foot of our hill, and all day ten or twelve little one-horse carriages stood there, wait-

ing to be hired. When the drivers saw us
coming down, they would all spring up on
their seats, and whip their horses, and drive
right at us, like an army making a charge,
holding up their whips, and shouting out,
"Signora, this is a good horse, this is a
good carriage, Signora," till sometimes we
were afraid of being run over. At last, I
made a rule that I would never take any one
who drove after me, and when they found
that out, they were more quiet. This night,
there was only one poor little carriage standing there; and the horse was so thin and
weak, he looked as if he were just ready to
die. Marianina looked at me with a very
sad face; she was afraid I would not be
willing to go in such a shabby carriage;
but I jumped in, and Marianina sang out to
the driver, "Go to the Piazza San Eustachio,
as fast as you can;" and then she laughed
out loud in spite of herself, she was so

pleased. She had never been out to the Twelfth Night Festa before.

The poor old horse did not draw us very far. He had not gone more than two-thirds of the way before he slipped down flat, and could not get up. The driver began to beat him cruelly; but I sprang out, and gave the man a small piece of money, and told him as well as I could, in my bad Italian, that he was a cruel man not to give his poor horse more to eat. What do you think he said? "Ah! Signora, he has more to eat than I have!"

Then I took tight hold of Marianina's hand, and we walked along with the crowd. Everybody was going toward San Eustachio. The crowd was pretty thick, even so far off as this; but it was no crowd at all in comparison with what it was when we got into the square itself. At first I was a little frightened. I did not like being pushed on all sides at once, and having one **boy blow a great whistle in** one of my ears, while another flapped **a great monkey-jack** up and **down under my nose.** But, **in a** few minutes, **I** saw **that they were all just as** good-natured **as they** could be, and that there really was **not** the slightest danger of getting hurt; so **I gave up minding** about **being pushed,** and then **I** had **as good** a time **as** Marianina. I wish I could **tell** you half the **things that** were **there to be** sold in those queer little out-door shops, with flaring tallow candles **or smoking** oil-lamps to see by. Every-thing you have ever **seen** in a toy-shop **in New York was** there; but of course **not** so nicely made. **There were stalls** full of games; stalls **full of books, and portfolios,** and stationery **of all sorts; great piles** and pyramids of **baskets,** with candles burning away **at top of** them, which it made you shudder **to** see, — **it** would be **so** easy for

one upset to kindle the whole in a blaze;
stalls of crockery; stalls of woollen scarfs,
and mittens, and comforters; stalls of plaster
images; stalls of cheap jewelry; stalls of
pictures of the Madonna and all the saints;
stalls of lamps; stalls of combs; stalls of
tin-ware, and stalls of iron; baby-houses,
and theatres, and fiddles, and donkeys on
wheels, and horses with tails made out of
hen's feathers, and noses painted blue,—oh!
how they would have made you laugh! The
prettiest stalls were the stalls of dolls; some
of them were arranged in rows of shelves,
one above another, high up in the air, on
which the dolls stood up, packed closely
side by side, as close as sardines in a
box. There were so many rows that the
upper row seemed almost out of sight, way
up in the dark. Others, who could not
afford to have nice wooden shelves, had
stuck two poles into the ground, and swung

cords across from pole to pole, and tied their dolls by the necks on these cords; there they swung back and forth, the poor hung dollies, and looked very uncomfortable. In front of the rows of dolls were rows of drums, and on the drums were bells; but nobody could tell me why drums and bells always went with the dolls.

Then there were other people with things to sell, who could not afford even two poles and a string, so they spread theirs down on the ground, and had a few bits of candles stuck in tins to light up their show. It proved how good-natured the Italians are, that this whole crowd took the greatest possible pains to turn out for these poor little spreads of things, and never trod on them. I noticed one old woman sitting flat on the stones, by a dozen or two crockery plates; one boy with a few gay-colored cotton hand-

kerchiefs spread out on the pavement, and
another with a row of photograph albums.

Very many had large wooden trays swung
by a string round their necks, and loaded so
full of things that it would seem as if the
first step in such a crowd would spill them
all, but I did not see a single one tip over.
One boy had his tray full of salt-cellars,
and glass and china; others had funny figures and toys; others carried long sticks
strung full of a sort of jumble-cake, which
the Romans call "giambelli," and are very
fond of eating.

Now, I have left to the last the oddest thing
of all about this crowd; almost every man
and boy in it had a whistle, or a trumpet, or
a horn, or a drum, or a rattle, and blew, and
rattled, and beat, and screamed with all his
might, till the noise was something which
could not be described. What with the
rattles, and whistles, and drums, and horns,

and everybody's shouting and laughing, you could not hear yourself speak. You must not think it was only boys who did this; grown-up men liked it just as much, and blew and screamed quite as loud; neither was it confined to the Romans. Every now and then, I met a party of English or American people who had come out to see, and they were all blowing whistles and beating drums, just like the rest. One young gentleman whom I knew came up behind me, and blew in my ear such a blast from a great tin trumpet that I gave a jump, and nearly knocked poor little Marianina down.

I forgot, too, to say that more than half of the people carried torches; and as some of the stalls were set thick with rows of blazing candles, it was as light as day in some parts of the square, and then, again, in others it would be quite dark.

We went away at eleven o'clock, for I

was afraid to be there any later alone with
Marianina; but the fun always lasts until
two or three o'clock in the morning. Sometimes, about midnight, the Roman nobility
go into the square to look on, and see how
the people amuse themselves. They used
to throw money into the crowd to see them
scramble for it, but they do not do that
now.

When Marianina left me to go to bed, she
kissed my hand and almost cried, she was
so grateful for the pleasure of seeing the
Festa, and for the few things I had bought
for her.

"Grazzia, O grazzia, Signora mia. Felic-
issima notte!" she said. I wonder if that
will sound as pleasantly printed as it sounds
when the affectionate Italian women say it.
It means, "Thanks, thanks, my lady! The
happiest of nights to you!"

COLORADO SNOW-BIRDS.

I'LL tell you how the snow-birds come,
 Here in our Winter days;
They make me think of chickens,
 With their cunning little ways.

We go to bed at night, and leave
 The ground all bare and brown,
And not a single snow-bird
 To be seen in all the town.

But when we wake at morning
 The ground with snow is white,
And with the snow, the snow-birds
 Must have travelled all the night;

For the streets and yards are full of them,
 The dainty little things,
With snow-white breasts, and soft brown heads,
 And speckled russet wings.

Not here and there a snow-bird,
　As we see them at the East,
But in great flocks, like grasshoppers,
　By hundreds, at the least,

They push and crowd and jostle,
　And twitter as they feed,
And hardly lift their heads up,
　For fear to miss a seed.

What 'tis they eat, nobody seems
　To know or understand;
The seeds are much too fine to see,
　All sifted in the sand.

But winds last Summer scattered them,
　All thickly on these plains;
The little snow-birds have no barns,
　But God protects their grains.

They let us come quite near them,
　And show no sign of dread;
Then, in a twinkling, the whole flock
　Will flutter on ahead

8

A step or two, and light, and feed,
　And look demure and tame,
And then fly on again, and stop,
　As if it were a game.

Some flocks count up to thousands,
　I know, and when they fly,
Their tiny wings make rustle,
　As if a wind went by.

They go as quickly as they come,
　Go in a night or day;
Soon as the snow has melted off,
　The darlings fly away,

But come again, again, again,
　All Winter, with each snow;
Brave little armies, through the cold,
　Swift back and forth they go.

I always wondered where they lived
　In Summer, till last year
I stumbled on them in their home,
　High in the upper air;

'Way up among the clouds it was,
   A many thousand feet,
But on the mountain-side gay flowers
   Were blooming fresh and sweet.

Great pine-trees' swaying branches
   Gave cool and fragrant shade;
And here, we found, the snow-birds
   Their Summer home had made.

" Oh, lucky little snow-birds!"
   We said, "to know so well,
In Summer time and Winter time,
   Your destined place to dwell—

" To journey, nothing doubting,
   Down to the barren plains,
Where harvests are all over,
   To find your garnered grains!

" Oh, precious little snow-birds!
   If we were half as wise,
If we were half as trusting
   To the Father in the skies,—

" He would feed us, though the harvests
　　Had ceased throughout the land,
And hold us, all our lifetime,
　　In the hollow of his hand!"

THE WATER-WORKS OF HEILBRUN.

THE Chateau of Heilbrun is near Salzburg, in Austria. Chateau is only another name for house, though it does sound so grand. I have seen many chateaus which made very pretty pictures when they were photographed, but which were nothing in the world but tumble-down old houses, that we in America should not think nice to live in. But this house of Heilbrun is quite a good one, though it was built two hundred and fifty years ago. It was built by an old archbishop of Salzburg, whose name was Marcus Sitticus. He must have been as fond of playing with water as any boy in America, I am sure; for instead of spending his money in building a handsome house, he spent it on making all sorts of curious

water-works on his grounds. On every
path and in every grove there are stone
statues of men, figures of dogs and of
horses, all of which are throwing water out
of their mouths as hard as they can. You
cannot walk ten steps without coming on
some new kind of thing either to hold water
or to spout water; and there is so much
water dripping and trickling, and showering
about, that it seems as if you were out in a
rain.

But the most curious water-works are in a
part of the grounds which is kept locked
up, and under the care of a man called the
water-master. He keeps the keys, and
knows how to let on the water to make all
the machinery go. The day we went to
Heilbrun happened to be a "feast-day" for
the people (that is, a day on which they do
not work). So we had the good luck to go
in with a crowd of poor workingmen and

women; and it was almost as good fun to see them as it was to see the water-works.

The water-master was a droll little man, with a gray beard and a fat red face. He never laughed; but his eyes twinkled, and he watched us all the time to see what we thought of his show. When he heard that we were from America, he was very kind to us, and took great pains to put us in good places, where we could see well without being wet. Everybody in Europe loves America, because it is a free country. I mean all the poor people do. I do not wonder that so many of them come away from their homes to live with us. I should think they would all come, to get away from the kings.

The first place the water-master took us into was a great cave. It was so dark that at first we could hardly see to walk. Then in a few minutes it seemed to grow lighter, and we saw a great stone basin full of water. Mosses and ferns were growing up around it, and little fir-trees were set up against the side of the cave. In this basin were a great red lobster and a black dolphin, made of wood. The water-master went into a corner and touched some spring, and the lobster and dolphin both began to sail round and round in the basin as if they were alive. Sounds like the singing of all sorts of birds came from among the fir-trees; and then came the words " cuckoo, cuckoo," just as plainly as the cuckoo itself could have said it; and all this was done by machinery, which was moved by the water.

Then we went to another cave; and all there was to be seen in this was a huge stone face set in the wall, painted red and white, like a mask, and with enormous black eyes. I was just beginning to wonder what this could mean; when oh! what a jump we all gave,

to see it suddenly roll up its eyes, open its
mouth, and show a fiery red tongue, which
came out ever so far and turned up on the
nose, and then went back again into the
mouth. It was almost too ugly to look at;
and yet it was very droll, for the eyes kept
rolling up and the red tongue running out
as fast as they could. The peasants all
shouted and screamed with delight; this
pleased them much more than the lobster
and dolphin. Then the water-master made
us all stand back on each side of the cave;
and, before we could ask what for, out flew
little fine streams of water from all sides of
the cave, making it as wet in one minute as
if there had been a hard rain. Then, as the
peasants were going out of the cave, he
touched some other invisible springs, and
played jets of water right across the path
they were walking in. The water seemed
to come from the ground, from the grass,

from the air, from everywhere. But he took good care not to let it go on us; the peasants liked the fun of it, and only laughed. One old woman got very wet, for she could not go so fast as the others; but she did not seem to mind it.

Then he entered another gate; and we followed him through it into a pretty path, with trees and flowers on the right-hand side, and on the left-hand a narrow brook of water. Its sides were straight, like the sides of a candle; but the water ran very fast. On one side of this brook were built five little stone houses, very much like dog-houses, only about twice as large; and, instead of having a low arched door in front, the whole front side was open, so that we could look in.

In the first one were a grindstone, and two figures standing by it, a man and a woman. The man held a knife, and the

woman had hold of the handle of the grindstone. As soon as the water-master touched
a spring, the woman began to turn the grindstone, and the man began to sharpen the
knife ; and there they stood, bending and
turning and sharpening away as hard as if
they were real live people. The brook ran
along in front, as quiet and innocent-looking
as if it hadn't anything in the world to do
with the man and the woman at the grindstone ; and all the while it was a tiny stream,
forced up from the brook into the machinery
of their legs and arms, which kept them at
work.

The next house was a little grist-mill,
with all the wheels and stones and beams in
perfect imitation of a real one; and the
miller, all dusty and white, standing by a
hopper, which turned swiftly round and
round, and let a fine stream of flour run out

into the mouth of the bag below. This was the prettiest thing of all.

The next thing was intended to be very solemn; but it was only funny. There was an imitation tree, with the figure of a man tied to it. He was meant to look like one of the old martyrs; but he did not look enough like a real man to look like a martyr. Before him stood another figure of a man, with a long spear in his hand. He was the executioner. When the machinery was wound up, the executioners began to stick the spear into the martyr's side; once in so many seconds the spear went in, and once in so many seconds the spear came out, and all this time the martyr never stirred. This was so very different from the way it would be with a real man being killed, that it made us laugh more and more the longer we looked at it. But the poor men and women looked very sober; for they thought it must be the representation of some old saint who had been killed by the heathen, and I am afraid they thought we were wicked people to laugh.

Next came a little house which I am afraid I cannot describe to you so that you will seem to see it, it was so very strange. In the middle was a little lake of water; in the lake, an island; on the island, a rock; fastened by chains to the rock, was the figure of a woman. Then there was a thing meant to be a sea-monster. It looked a little like an elephant, a little like a grasshopper, a little like a turtle; but on the whole it did not look like anything! This monster came sailing slowly round the island; and, just as it got opposite the woman, and looked as if it were going to bite her, a door flew open, and out stepped the figure of a man in armor, with a bright brass sword in his hand. The sword gave a hack at the head of the monster; **but the** monster sailed on as if nothing had happened, **and came round** again from behind the **tree.** **Again** the **door flew open,** the man **in armor** stepped out, **the** sword hacked **at** the monster's head; and so they kept on sailing round and hacking, and sailing round and hacking, till we **all** laughed so we could hardly stand. The peasants **did** not laugh so much, **for they** did not understand it, and I dare say they thought it **must be** a representation of a saint being killed. But it was **taken from** an **old** fable. The woman's **name** was Andromeda; **and the story was** that she was bound **to a rock, to** be eaten **up** by a horrible **monster, and** a great hero **came and** killed the monster, and set her free.

The next house was a pretty **little dairy.** Pans **of** milk and cream setting on the shelves; pats of butter in **piles on plates;** and a figure of a man churning **with a** wooden churn, which made a spattering noise quite like a real churn.

This was the last of the little stone houses.

Now we came to the greatest curiosity of all: a large chamber hollowed out in the rock, and two great folding-doors on the side toward the path. When these were thrown open, there we saw in the centre of the chamber a tower three stories high, full of windows, and with galleries running around it. This was meant, we thought, for a sort of palace; many men and women were looking out of the windows, and standing on the galleries.

Around the walls of the chamber were also galleries, with pillars at the front, and divided off into rooms. In each room there was a representation of some trade, or some sort of store; and men and women at work at the trade, or selling goods in the store. The floor of the chamber was crowded with figures as the streets of a city are; in fact, the whole thing was intended to represent a town, with its inhabitants all engaged about their business.

The water-master let us look at it for some time before he set it in motion. Then he went across the path to a high wooden box, lifted up the lid, and did something with a key,—we could not see what; but in one second every figure in the town began to move. The people in the windows of the tower turned their heads from side to side, and looked as if they were talking with each other. The King on the balcony took off his hat and bowed to the people below. The baker began to knead his bread; the shoemaker to hammer on his last; the butcher knocked an ox on the head to kill it; the ox plunged down on its knees as if dead, but got up on his legs in a half second, all ready to be killed again when the time

came round. There was a tavern, with two
men sitting at dinner, and one of them
laughing so that he bent back almost double.
There was a beautiful little store, with silks
and ribbons and stockings and laces, all
hanging at the windows and in the door;
and the storekeeper himself, standing on the
threshold, stretching out his hands to invite
the people to come in. There was an old
woman being wheeled about in a wheel-
barrow; and another old woman, funniest of
all, who was running wildly up and down in
the crowd, shaking her head and looking as
if she were crazy. Then there were brick-
layers going up ladders, with hods full of
bricks on their shoulders; carpenters upon the
roof of a house, hammering at the shingles;
workmen with a derrick, lifting up stones.
In short, I might as well tell you that there
is nothing that you have ever seen workmen
doing in the streets of a city which this old

9

Marcus Sitticus, the Archbishop, had not contrived to get into this great toy-house of his. While these things were going on, there was also music, like the music of an organ, coming from nobody could see where; but it was made on some hidden instrument, which was played by the water. Still the little brook went trotting along at our feet, as unconcerned as if it had no share in all this wonderful machinery.

The peasants were quite silent while they looked at this. Over the other things they had laughed and shouted; but this was too mysterious for them. I think they were a little afraid of it. I thought it very strange they had not brought their little children with them to see these things. There was not a single child there.

The last sight of all was the most beautiful. We went into another great dark cave; and here, on a round stone table, lay a gilt

crown. Who could imagine what this had
to do with water-works? Presently the
crown rose slowly up in the air, though
nobody's hands touched it. The stone table
had holes in it, and through these holes five
streams of water were being forced up, and
they lifted the crown. Higher and higher
and higher it went, until it reached nearly
the top of the cave; and there it hovered,
gently rising and falling on the top of the
shining fountain of water. Then the fountain slowly sank, lowering the crown, till it
lay on the table again. Three times we
saw it rise and fall, and each time it looked
more beautiful than before. The peasants
clapped their hands with delight, and so did
we. Then we gave the good-natured water-
master some money, and walked back through
the shady path, past the little town, and
the mill, and the dairy, and the martyr,
and Andromeda. They were all as still

as midnight; and the little figures looked droller than ever, standing so quietly. Only the crazy old woman, in the streets of the little town, still shook her head; and we took the liberty of giving her a tap on the cheek as we passed.

The water-master opened the gate for us, and stood smiling and bowing his red face as long as we were in sight. "Good-by, Kuhleborn," said we; but he did not know what we meant; and neither will you, unless you ask some kind friend to tell you the beautiful German story of Undine, who had an uncle called Kuhleborn, that lived in the sea and ruled all the brooks and rivers.

MORNING-GLORY.

WONDROUS interlacement!
  Holding fast to threads by green and
silky rings,
With the dawn it spreads its white and purple
   wings;
Generous in its bloom, and sheltering while it
  clings,
   Sturdy morning-glory.

   Creeping through the casement,
Slanting to the floor in dusty, shining beams,
Dancing on the door, in quick fantastic gleams
Comes the new day's light, and pours in tideless
   streams,
   Golden morning-glory.

   In the lowly basement,
Rocking in the sun, the baby's cradle stands.
Now the little one thrusts out his rosy hands;
Soon his eyes will open; then in all the lands
   No such morning-glory.

CHILDREN'S PREACHING IN THE CHURCH OF ARA CŒLI, IN ROME.

ARA CŒLI is the name of one of the oldest churches in Rome. It is at the top of a high hill, and to get to it you have to go up a flight of more than a hundred stone steps. These steps are as old as Rome is, and Julius Cæsar himself went up them many a time; for in his day there was a temple to Jupiter where the church of **Ara Cœli** now stands, and all the Roman emperors and generals used to go there to give thanks to Jupiter whenever they had a victory. In this church the little Roman children preach sermons, every afternoon, from Christmas until Twelfth Night, and once I heard a little girl preach there. As I went up the long flight of stone stairs, I passed many Roman men and women sitting there, with all sorts of odd and useless things to sell, — old bits of money, which they pretended were ancient relics, and pictures of saints, which they said would keep me from all harm if I would only buy them. At every step, somebody on my right hand, or on my left, screamed out: "O Signora! see this fine picture for one baioccho" (that is about one cent); or, "O Signora! here is good luck for you and the Sacred Heart of Mary, for one baioccho," till I thought I should never get away from them all. On the top step sat a poor old beggar, such as one sees every day in Rome, holding a tin box with a hole in it, through which people drop money. The beggars do not speak a word, but they shake this box furiously as you pass them, jingling the coin to let you hear how much money other people have given them; and it

is strange how apt the sound of this money
is to make you think you will drop in a
little piece more. After I had given the
beggar a copper, I went into the church. I
remember that I got stuck fast in the
door, and a good-natured soldier helped me
through. This was not because I was too
big for the door; but all the Roman churches
have great thick leather curtains swung in
their doors, — the door itself stands wide
open; but this great curtain, which is as
heavy as a mattress, and looks more like
one than like anything else, is hung from
the top of the doorway, like a second door,
and it takes a strong push to shove it in far
enough for a person to squeeze through the
opening.

Away down at one end of the church was
a large square table, covered with a red
cloth; behind the table was a little step-
ladder leading up to it; and round the table

had already gathered a large crowd of people. Presently a man came out of a side-door, leading a little girl, who did not look more than five years old. He helped her to climb up on the table, and then he sat down on the top step of the ladder, so as to be near her. He was her father, and he was very proud of her. The little girl ran into the middle of the table, and made a funny bow, something like the bows monkey-jacks make when you pull the wires. Then she opened her little bit of a mouth, and out of it came the very littlest bit of a voice you ever heard; it sounded as fine as the finest squeak a violin can make. I suppose her voice was really as loud as other little girls' voices; but it could not make any noise in that great stone church.

She wore a black and red striped woollen gown, made just like an old woman's gown — long, with a tight, straight waist, and tight, long sleeves; she had a row of coral beads around her neck, and her hair was braided up tight, and wound round and round in a small knot at the back of her head with a big comb, such as grown-up people wear. She had on dark leggins and low shoes; and altogether she was the drollest, most old-fashioned-looking little body I ever saw. She looked as if she might have been Cinderella's little old fairy godmother, only she was not quite fine enough. But she had learned her sermon perfectly; she knew it so well, and said it so fast, that she kept getting out of breath every few minutes, and had to stop right in the middle of a sentence, or anywhere, to draw more air into her lungs.

She made many gestures with her little arms, and sometimes held up her little bit of a forefinger, and shook it with a threatening shake, which it was enough to make anybody shout out loud with laughter to see. I think the finger might have been about an inch and a half long. I could not understand what she said; I thought this was because I knew so little Italian; but some of my friends, who spoke Italian very well, were there, and they could not understand any better than I did. However, we made out enough to know that she was telling us that if we did not obey Jesus we should all go, when we died, to a dreadful place, where there were flames of fire to burn us for hundreds and hundreds of years. At the end of her sermon she spread out her arms as wide as she could, and said; "Farewell, my dear friends! I hope we shall all meet in heaven, in the presence of the Holy Virgin Mary, and be very happy always." Then she made another funny little bow, and jumped off the table. Her father caught her in his arms, and carried her over to the other side of the church, to see the sacred Bambino. We all followed him, and crowded up around her, and some of the ladies gave her money. The father said her name was Isabella, and she was six years old, although she looked so young and was so small. The nuns in a convent where she went to school had taught her this little sermon, and it had taken her three whole weeks to learn it. He was so proud of her, and so pleased that she had preached her sermon so well, that he kept kissing her over and over, and smiling at all of us, as if he had known us all our lives. He was only a poor workingman, and I suppose it was the greatest pleasure of his whole year to have this little girl of his preach a sermon in Ara Cœli, and be praised and admired by the foreign gentlemen and ladies.

But now I must tell you what is the sacred Bambino, which we all went to look at after the sermon was ended. "Bambino" is Italian for "little baby;" and the sacred Bambino is a doll which is dressed to represent Jesus Christ when he was a little baby. It is kept either sitting or lying in the lap of a large wax figure of a woman who is called the Virgin Mary, Christ's mother. Every Roman Catholic Church has these figures, and I presume you may have seen them in America. But no church in Rome has so fine a Bambino as this in Ara Cœli, nor one of which such wonderful stories are told. The monks say that it was carved out of wood which grew on the Mount of Olives, and that St. Luke himself painted its face. They have made the Romans believe that it has a miraculous power to cure diseases, and it is often sent for where people are very ill. When it is being carried through the streets, very good Roman Catholics go down on their knees, or, at least, make the sign of the cross. Sometimes they run along after the carriage, and try to touch the wheels, crying out: "O most blessed Bambino! keep us well; O holy Bambino! give us thy blessing."

Twenty years ago there was a great revolution in Rome, and some of the people who did not like the Pope and his cardinals, burnt up the fine red coaches which the cardinals rode in. They were just going to burn the Pope's, too; but somebody proposed that, instead of burning it, they should give it to the sacred Bambino of Ara Cœli.

This pleased the people very much; for although they hated to be ruled over and oppressed by the cardinals, they were very good Roman Catholics at heart. So they drew the coach up to Ara Cœli, and the monks put the Bambino in it, and drove through all the chief streets of Rome, to let

everybody know what had been done with
the Pope's carriage.

Think of a wooden doll, about as big as a
baby three months old, dressed all in laces
and tinsel and diamonds, with a gold crown
of most precious jewels on its head, being
taken out to ride in a coach, and carried into
the rooms of sick people, that they might be
cured by looking at it!

But the oddest story of the Bambino of
Ara Cœli is about its having once been
carried off. The monks tell this story as if
they believed it. Perhaps some of them do,
though it is hard enough to see how they can.
They say that many years ago, there was an
English woman in Rome who fell in love
with the Bambino, and used to come every
day to the church, and sit for long hours
looking at it. At last, she wanted so much
to have it for her own, that she had another
doll made exactly like it, and took that to

the church, and watched and waited for an opportunity, when no one was near, to change them, — putting her common doll into the lap of the Virgin Mary, and carrying off the sacred Bambino for herself. All the rest of that day, nobody noticed the change ; but at midnight all the bells of the church and of the convent adjoining it began to ring. The monks were frightened enough — as well they might be — to find all their bells ringing furiously, and no human hands touching the ropes. They ran into the church, and opened the door at the top of the stone steps, and there stood the sacred Bambino, waiting to be let in ! What became of the English woman, the story does not say ; but that is the true story, as many a little Roman boy and girl would tell you, of the Sacred Bambino of Ara Cœli.

"THE PENNY YE MEANT TO GI'E."

THERE'S a funny tale of a stingy man,
    Who was none too good, but might have
      been worse,
Who went to his church on a Sunday night,
    And carried along his well-filled purse.

When the sexton came with his begging-plate,
    The church was but dim with the candle's light:
The stingy man fumbled all through his purse,
    And chose a coin by touch and not sight.

It's an odd thing now that guineas should be
    So like unto pennies in shape and size.
"I'll give a penny," the stingy man said;
    "The poor must not gifts of pennies despise."

The penny fell down with a clatter and ring!
    And back in his seat leaned the stingy man.
"The world is so full of the poor," he thought,
    "I can't help them all, — I give what I can."

Ha, ha! how the sexton smiled, to be sure,
    To see the gold guinea fall in his plate!
Ha, ha! how the stingy man's heart was wrung,
    Perceiving his blunder, but just too late!

10

"No matter," he said; "in the Lord's account
  That guinea of gold is set down to me.
They lend to Him who give to the poor;
  It will not so bad an investment be."

"Na, na, mon," the chuckling sexton cried out,
  "The Lord is na cheated — He kens thee well;
He knew it was only by accident
  That out o' thy fingers the guinea fell!

"He keeps an account, na doubt, for the puir;
  But in that account He'll set down to thee
Na mair o' that golden guinea, my mon,
  Than the one bare penny ye meant to gi'e!"

There's a comfort, too, in the little tale —
  A serious side as well as a joke;
A comfort for all the generous poor,
  In the comical words the sexton spoke.

A comfort to think that the good Lord knows
  How generous we really desire to be,
And will give us credit in His account,
  For all the pennies we long "to gi'e."

A PARABLE.

ONCE there was born a man with a great genius for painting and sculpture. It was not in this world that he was born, but in a world very much like this in some respects, and very different in others. The world in which this great genius was born was governed by a beneficent and wise Ruler, who had such wisdom, and such power, that he decided, before each being was born, for what purpose he would best be fitted in life; he then put him in the place best suited to the work he was to do; and he gave into his hands a set of instruments to do the work with.

There was one peculiarity about these instruments: they could never be replaced; on this point this great and wise Ruler was inexorable. He said to every being who was born into his realms :

"Here is your set of instruments to work with ; if you take good care of them, they will last a lifetime ; if you let them get rusty or broken, you can perhaps have them brightened up a little, or mended ; but they will never be as good as new, and you can never have another set. Now you see how important it is that you keep them always in good order."

This man of whom I speak had a complete set of all the tools necessary for a sculptor's work, and also a complete set of painters' brushes and colors. He was a wonderful man ; for he could make very beautiful statues, and he could also paint very beautiful pictures. He became, while he was very young, famous ; and everybody wanted something that he had carved or painted.

Now I do not know whether it was that he did not believe what the good Ruler told him about his set of instruments, or whether he did not care to keep on working any longer; but this is what happened: he grew very careless about his brushes, and let his tools lie out over night where it was damp. He left some of his brushes full of paint for weeks, and the paint dried in, so that when at last he tried to wash it out, out came the bristles by dozens, and the brushes were entirely ruined. The dampness of the night air rusted the edges of some of his very finest tools, and the things which he had to use to clean off the rust were so powerful, that they ate into the fine metal of the tools, and left the edges so uneven that they would no longer make fine strokes.

However, he kept on painting, and making statues, and doing the best he could

with the few and imperfect tools he had
left.   But people began to say, "What is
the matter with this man's pictures? and
what is the matter with his statues? He
does not do half as good work as he used
to!"

Then he was very angry, and said the
people were only envious and malicious;
that he was the same he always had been;
and his pictures and statues were as good as
ever.   But he could not make anybody
else think so.   They all knew better.

One day the Ruler sent for him, and said
to him :

"Now you have reached the prime of
your life; it is time that you should do
some really great work. I want a grand
statue made for the gate-way of one of
my cities. Here is the design. Take it
home and study it, and see if you can
undertake to execute it."

As soon as the poor sculptor studied the design, his heart sank within him; there were several parts of it which required the finest workmanship of one of his most delicate instruments; that instrument was entirely ruined by rust; the edge was all eaten away in notches. In vain he tried all possible devices to bring it again to a fine, sharp edge. Nothing could be done with it. The most experienced workmen shook their heads as soon as they saw it, and said:

"No, no, sir! it is too late; if you had brought it to us at first, we might possibly have made it sharp enough for you to use a little while with great care; but it is past help now." Then he ran frantically around the country, trying to borrow a similar instrument from some one. But one of the most remarkable peculiarities about these sets of instruments given by the Ruler of this world I am speaking of was, that they were of no use at all in the hands of anybody except the one to whom the Ruler had given them. Several of the sculptor's friends were so sorry for him, that they offered him their instruments in place of his own; but he tried in vain to use them. They were not fitted to his hand; he could not make the kind of stroke he wanted to make with them. So he went sadly back to the Ruler, and said:

"Oh, sir, I am most unhappy! I cannot execute this beautiful design for your statue."

"But why cannot you execute it?" said the Ruler.

"Alas, sir!" replied the unfortunate man, "by some sad accident one of my finest tools was so rusted that it cannot be restored. Without that tool, it is impossible to make this statue."

Then the Ruler looked very severely at him, and said:

"Oh, Sculptor! accidents very seldom happen to the wise and careful. But you are also a painter, I believe. Perhaps you can paint the picture I wish to have painted immediately, for my new palace. Here is the drawing of it. Go home and study this. This also will be an opportunity worthy of your genius."

The poor fellow was not much comforted by this; for he remembered that he had not even looked at his brushes for a long time. However, he took the sketch, thanked the Ruler, and withdrew.

It proved to be the same with the sketch for the picture, as it had been with the design for the statue; it required the finest workmanship in parts of it, and the brushes which were needed for this had been long ago destroyed; only their handles remained. How did the painter regret his folly as he picked up the old defaced handles from the floor, and looked at them hopelessly ! Again he went to the Ruler, and, with still greater embarrassment than **before**, acknowledged that he was unable to paint the picture, because he had not the proper brushes. This time the Ruler looked at him with terrible severity, and spoke in a **voice** of the sternest displeasure.

" What, then, do you expect **to** do, sir, for the rest of your life, **if your** instruments are in such a condition ? "

" Alas, sir, I do **not** know ! " replied the poor man, covered with confusion.

" **You** deserve **to starve,**" said the **Ruler** ; and ordered the servants to show him out of the palace.

After this, matters went from bad to worse with the painter ; every **few days,** some one of his instruments broke under his **hand ;** they had been so poorly taken care of, that **they did not last** half as long as they **were** meant to. His work grew poorer and poorer, until he fell so low that he was forced to eke out a miserable living by painting the walls of the commonest houses, and making the coarsest kind of water-jars out of clay. Finally his last instrument failed him; he had nothing left to work with; and as he had for many years done only very coarse and cheap work, and had not been able to lay up any money, he was driven to beg his food from door to door, and finally died of hunger.

This is the end of the Parable. Next comes the Moral. Now, please don't skip all the rest, because it is called "Moral." It will not be very long. I wish I had called my story a Conundrum instead of a Parable, and then the moral would have been the answer. How that would have puzzled you all, — a conundrum so many pages long! And I wonder how many of you would have

guessed the true answer? How many of
you would have thought enough about your
own bodies, to have seen that they were
only sets of instruments given to you to
work with? The Parable is a truer one than
you think, at first; but the longer you think,
the more you will see how true it is. Are
we not each of us born into the world provided with one body, and only one, which
must last us as long as we live in this world?
Is it not by means of this body that we feel,
learn, and accomplish everything? Is it not
a most wonderful and beautiful set of instruments? Can we ever replace any one of
them? Can we ever have any one of them
made as good as new, after it has once been
seriously out of order? In one respect the
Parable is not a true one, for the Parable
tells the story of a man whose set of instruments was adapted to only two uses, — to
sculpture and to painting. But it would not

be easy to count up all the things which human beings can do by help of these wonderful bodies in which they live. Think, for a moment, of all the things you do in any one day: all the breathing, eating, drinking, and running, of all the thinking, speaking, feeling, learning, you do in any one day. Now if any one of the instruments is seriously out of order, you cannot do one of these things so well as you know how to do it.

When any one of the instruments is very seriously out of order, there is always pain. If the pain is severe, you can't think of anything else while it lasts; all your other instruments are of no use to you, just because of the pain in that one which is out of order. If the pain and the disordered condition last a great while, the instrument is so injured that it is never again so strong as it was in the beginning. All the doctors

in the world cannot make it so. Then you
begin to be what people call an invalid;
that is, a person who doesn't have the full
use of any one part of his body; who is
never exactly comfortable himself, and who
is likely to make everybody about him more
or less uncomfortable.

I do not know anything in this world half
so strange as the way in which people
neglect their bodies: that is, their set of
instruments; their one set of instruments
which they can never replace, and can do
very little towards mending. When it is
too late, when the instruments are hopelessly out of order, then they do not neglect
them any longer; then they run about
frantically, as the poor sculptor did, trying
to find some one to help him; and this is
one of the saddest sights in the world, — a
man or a woman running from one climate
to another climate, and from one doctor to

another doctor, trying to cure or patch up a body that is out of order.

Now, perhaps you will say this is a dismal and unnecessary sermon to preach to young people; they have their fathers and mothers to take care of them; they don't take care of themselves. Very true; but fathers and mothers cannot be always with their children; fathers and mothers cannot always make their children remember and obey their directions. More than all, it is very hard to make children realize that it is of any great importance that they should keep all the laws of health. I know when I was a little girl, when people said to me you must not do thus and thus, for if you do you will take cold, I used to think, "Who cares for a little cold? Supposing I do catch one!" and when I was shut up in the house for several days with a bad sore throat, and suffered horrible pain, I never reproached myself. I thought that sore throats must come now and then, whether or no, and that I must take my turn. But now I have learned, that if no law of health were ever broken we need never have a day's illness, might grow old in entire freedom from suffering, and gradually fall asleep at last, instead of dying terrible deaths from disease; and I am all the while wishing that I had known it when I was young. If I had known it, I'll tell you what I would have done: I would have just tried the experiment, at any rate, of never doing a single thing which could, by any possibility, get any one of the instruments of my body out of order. I wish I could see some boy or girl try it, yet: never to sit up late at night; never to have a close, bad air in the room; never to sit with wet feet; never to wet them, if it were possible to help it; never to go out in the cold weather without

being properly wrapped up; never to go
out of a hot room into the cold out-door air,
without throwing some extra wrap on; never
to eat or drink an unwholesome thing; never
to touch tea, or coffee, or candy, or pie-
crust; never to let a day pass without at
least two good hours of exercise in the open
air; never to read a word by twilight, or in
the cars; never to let the sun be shut out
of rooms. This is a pretty long list of
"nevers," but "never" is the only word that
conquers. "Once in a while," is the very
watchword of temptation and defeat. I do
believe that the "once in a while" things
have ruined more bodies, and more souls,
too, than all the other things put together.
Moreover, the "never" way is easy, and the
"once in a while" way is hard. After you
have once made up your mind "never" to
do a certain thing, that is the end of it, if
you are a sensible person. But if you only

11

say "this is a bad habit," or "this is a dangerous indulgence, I will be a little on my guard, and not do it too often," you have put yourself in the most uncomfortable of all positions ; the temptation will knock at your door twenty times a-day, and you will have to be fighting the same old battles over and over again, as long as you live. This is especially true in regard to the matter of which I have been speaking to you,—the care of the body. When you have once laid down to yourself the laws you mean to keep, the things you will always do, and the things you will "*never*" do, then your life arranges itself in a system at once ; and you are not interrupted and hindered as the undecided people are, by wondering what is best, or safe, or wholesome, or too unwholesome, at different times.

Don't think it would be a sort of slavery to give up so much for sake of keeping your body in order. It is the only real freedom, though at first it does not look so much like freedom as the other way. It is the sort of freedom of which some poet sung once. I never knew who he was. I heard the lines only once, and have forgotten all except the last three, but I think of those every day. He was speaking of the true freedom which there is in keeping the laws of nature, and he said it was like the freedom of the true poet, who —

> " Always sings
> In strictest bonds of rhyme and rule,
> And finds in them not bonds, but wings."

I think the difference between a person who has kept all the laws of health, and thereby has a good strong sound body, that can carry him wherever he wants to go, and do whatever he wants to do, and a person who has let his body get all out of order so that

he has to lie in bed half his time and suffer,
is quite as great a difference as there is
between a creature with wings and a creature without wings!

Don't you?

And this is the end of the Moral.

MY BROKEN-WINGED BIRD.

FOR days I have been cherishing
    A little bird with broken wing.
I love it in my heart of hearts;
To win its love I try all arts;
I call it by each sweet pet name
That I can think, its fear to tame.
My room is still and bright and warm;
The little thing is safe from harm.
If I had left it where it lay
Fluttering in the wintry day,
No mate remaining by its side,
Before nightfall it must have died.
It sips the drink, it eats the food;
Plenty of both, all sweet and good.
But all the while my hand it flies,
Looks up at me with piteous eyes;
From morn till night, restless and swift,
Runs to and fro, and tries to lift
Itself upon its broken wing,
And through the window-pane to spring.

Poor little bird!   Myself I see
From morn till night in watching thee.
A Power I cannot understand
Is sheltering me with loving hand;
It calls me by the dearest name,
My love to win, my fear to tame;
Each day my daily food provides,
And night and day from danger hides
Me safe: the food, the warmth, I take,
Yet all the while ungrateful make   .
Restless and piteous complaints,
And strive to break the kind restraints.

Dear little bird, 'twill not be long;
Each day thy wing is growing strong;
When it is healed, and thou canst fly,
My windows will be opened high;
And I shall watch with loving eyes
To see thee soar in sunny skies.
I, too, some day, on healèd wing
Set free, shall soar aloft and sing,
And in my joy no memory find
Of prison-walls I left behind.

CHEERY PEOPLE.

OH, the comfort of them! There is but one thing like them, — that is sunshine. It is the fashion to state the comparison the other end foremost — *i. e.* to flatter the cheery people by comparing them to the sun. I think it is the best way of praising the sunshine, to say that it is almost as bright and inspiring as the presence of cheery people.

That the cheery people are brighter and better even than sunshine is very easily proved; for who has not seen a cheery person make a room and a day bright in spite of the sun's not shining at all, — in spite of clouds and rain and cold all doing their very best to make it dismal? There-

fore I say, the fair way is to compare the
sun to cheery people, and not cheery people
to the sun. However, whichever way we
state the comparison, it is a true and good
one; and neither the cheery people nor the
sun need take offence. In fact, I believe
they will always be such good friends, and
work so steadily together for the same ends,
that there is no danger of either's grudging
the other the credit of what has been done.
The more you think of it, the more you see
how wonderfully alike the two are in their
operation on the world. The sun on the
fields makes things grow — fruits and flowers
and grains; the cheery person in the house
makes everybody do his best, — makes the
one who can sing feel like singing, and the
one who has an ugly, hard job of work to
do, feel like shouldering it bravely and
having it over with. And the music and
mirth and work in the house, are they not

like the flowers and fruits and grains in the field?

The sun makes everybody glad. Even the animals run and leap, and seem more joyous when it shines out; and no human being can be so gross-grained, or so ill, that he does not brighten up a little when a great broad, warm sunbeam streams over him and plays on his face. It is just so with a cheery person. His simple presence makes even animals happier. Dogs know the difference between him and a surly man. When he pats them on the head and speaks to them, they jump and gambol about him just as they do in the sunshine. And when he comes into the room where people are ill, or out of sorts, or dull and moping, they brighten up, spite of themselves, just as they do when a sudden sunbeam pours in, — only more so; for we often see people so ill they do not care whether the sun shines or not, or so cross that they do not even see whether the sun shines **or** not ; **but I** have never yet seen anybody so cross or so ill that the voice and face of a cheery person would **not make** them brighten up a little.

If there were only a sure and certain recipe for making a cheery **person, how** glad we would all be **to try it !   How thank-**ful we would **all be to do good like sunshine !** To cheer everybody up, and help everybody along ! — to have everybody's **face brighten** the minute we came in sight !   **Why, it seems to me** that there cannot be in this life **any** pleasure half so great as this would **be. If we looked at life** only from a selfish point of view, **it would be worth while to** be a cheery person, merely **because it** would be such a satisfaction to **have everybody** so glad to live with us, to see us, even to meet us 'on the street.

People who have done things which have

made them famous, such as winning great
battles or filling high offices, often have
what are called "ovations." Hundreds of
people get together and make a procession,
perhaps, or go into a great hall and make
speeches, all to show that they recognize
what the great man has done. After he
is dead, they build a stone monument to him,
perhaps, and celebrate his birthday for a few
years. Men work very hard sometimes for
a whole lifetime to earn a few things of this
sort. But how much greater a thing it
would be for a man to have every man,
woman, and child in his own town know
and love his face because it was full of
kindly good cheer! Such a man has a
perpetual "ovation," year in and year out,
whenever he walks on the street, whenever he enters a friend's house.

"I jist likes to let her in at the door,"
said an Irish servant one day, of a woman I

know whose face was always cheery and bright; "the face of her does one good, shure!"

I said if there were only a recipe—a sure and certain recipe—for making a cheery person, we would all be glad to try it. There is no such recipe, and perhaps if there were, it is not quite certain that we would all try it. It would take time and trouble. Cheeriness cannot be taught, like writing, "in twenty lessons;" nor analyzed and classified and set forth in a manual, such as "The Art of Polite Conversation," or "Etiquette Made Easy for Ladies and Gentlemen." It lies so deep that no surface-rules of behavior, no description ever so minute of what it is or is not, does or does not do, can ever enable a person to "take it up" and "master" it, like a trade or a study. I believe that it is, in the outset, a good gift from God at one's birth, very much dependent on one's body, and a thing to be more profoundly grateful for than all that genius ever inspired, or talent ever accomplished. This is natural, spontaneous, inevitable cheeriness. This, if we were not born with it, we cannot have. But next best to this is deliberate, intended, and persistent cheeriness, which we can create, can cultivate, and can so foster and cherish, that after a few years the world will never suspect that it was not a hereditary gift handed down to us from generations. To do this we have only to watch the cheeriest people we know, and follow their example. We shall see, first, that the cheery person never minds — or if he minds, never says a word about — small worries, vexations, perplexities. Second, that he is brimful of sympathy in other people's gladness; he is heartily, genuinely glad of every bit of good luck or joy which comes to other people. Thirdly, he has a keen sense of

humor, and **never** lets any **droll** thing escape
him ; he **thinks it** worth **while to** laugh, and
to make everybody about him laugh, **at every**
amusing thing ; **no** matter how small, he has
his laugh, and **a** good hearty laugh too, and
tries to make everybody share it. Patience,
sympathy, and humor, — these are the **three**
most manifest **traits in the cheery person.**
But there **is** something else, which **is more**
an emotion than a **trait, more a** state of
feeling than a quality **of mind.** This **is**
lovingness. This is the secret, so far as
there **is a secret;** this **is the** real **point of**
difference between the mirth of the witty
and **sarcastic person, which does us no** good,
and **the mirth of the** cheery **person, which**
"doeth good **like a** medicine."

Somebody once asked **a great** painter,
whose pictures were remarkable **for their**
exquisite and beautiful coloring, "Pray, **Mr.**
——, **how** do you **mix your** colors?"

"With brains, madam — with brains," growled the painter. His ill-nature spoke a truth. All men had or might have the colors he used; but no man produced the colors he produced.

So I would say of cheeriness. Patience, sympathy, and humor are the colors; but patience may be mere doggedness and reticence, sympathy may be wordy and shallow and selfish, and humor may be only a sharp perception of the ridiculous. Only when they are mixed with love — love, three times love — do we have the true good cheer of genuine cheery people.

A SHORT CATECHISM.

A^T sunset of a summer's day,
   All curled up in a funny heap,
Beneath the currant-bushes lay
   A boy named Willy, half asleep.

But peeping through his sleepy eyes
   He watched all things as if he dreamed,
And did not feel the least surprise
   However strange and queer they seemed.

And every creature going by
   He hailed with questions from the grass,
And laughed and called out sleepily,
   "Unless you answer you can't pass."

"O caterpillar, now tell me
   Why you roll up so tight and round;
You are the drollest thing to see,
   A hairy marble on the ground."

" I roll me up to save my bones
    When I fall down; young man, if you
  Could do the same, the stumps and stones
    Would never bruise you black and blue."

" O spider, tell me why you hide
    The ropes and ladders which you spin,
  And keep them all locked up inside
    Your little body slim and thin."

" I hide my ropes and ladders fine
    Away from neighbors' thievish greed;
  If you kept yours as I keep mine,
    You'd always have one when you need."

" Why do you buzz so, busy bee?
    Why don't you make your honey still?
  You move about so boisterously,
    I'm sure you must much honey spill."

" I buzz and buzz, you silly boy,
    Because I can work better so;
  Just as you whistle for pure joy
    When on the road to school you go."

12

"O robin, wicked robin, why
    Did you my mamma's cherries eat?
  You thought no mortal soul was nigh;
    But I saw you from bill to feet."

"And I saw you, my fine young lad,
    And waited till you'd left the tree;
  I thought when you your fill had had,
    There would be little left for me!"

"O big bull-frogs, why do you make
    Such ugly noises every night!
  Nobody can a half-nap take;
    You make our baby cry with fright."

"O Willy, we suppose the noise
    Is not a pleasant noise to hear;
  But we've one hundred little boys, —
    Frog-boys so cunning and so dear;

"And it is not an easy task,
    You may believe, to put to beds
  A hundred little frogs who ask
    All questions which pop in their heads."

THE FROG BOYS.

THE EXPRESSION OF ROOMS.

ROOMS have just as much expression as faces. They produce just as strong an impression on us at first sight. The instant we cross the threshold of a room, we know certain things about the person who lives in it. The walls and the floor, and the tables and chairs all speak out at once, and betray some of their owner's secrets. They tell us whether she is neat or unneat, orderly or disorderly, and, more than all, whether she is of a cheerful, sunny temperament, and loves beauty in all things, or is dull and heavy, and does not know pretty things from ugly ones. And just as these traits in a person act on us, making us happy. and cheerful, or gloomy and sad, so does the room act upon us. We may not know, perhaps, what it is that is raising or depressing our spirits; we may not suspect that we could be influenced by such a thing; but it is true, nevertheless.

I have been in many rooms in which it was next to impossible to talk with any animation or pleasure, or to have any sort of good time. They were dark and dismal; they were full of ugly furniture, badly arranged; the walls and the floors were covered with hideous colors; no two things seemed to belong together, or to have any relation to each other; so that the whole effect on the eye was almost as torturing as the effect on the ear would be of hearing a band of musicians playing on bad instruments, and all playing different tunes.

I have also been in many rooms where you could not help having a good time, even if there were nothing especial going on in the way of conversation or amusement, just because the room was so bright and cosey. It did you good simply to sit still there. You almost thought you would like to go sometimes when the owner was away, and you need not talk with anybody but the room itself.

In very many instances the dismal rooms were the rooms on which a great deal of money had been spent, and the cosey rooms belonged to people who were by no means rich. Therefore, since rooms can be made cosey and cheerful with very little money, I think it is right to say that it is every woman's duty to make her rooms cosey and cheerful. I do not forget that, in speaking to my readers, I am speaking to girls who are for the most part living in their parents' houses, and who have not, therefore, the full control of their own rooms. But it is precisely during these years of life that the habits and tastes are formed; and the girl who allows her own room in her father's house to be untidy and unadorned, will inevitably, if she ever has a house of her own, let that be untidy and unadorned too.

There is not one of my readers, I am sure, who does not have, in the course of the year, pocket-money enough to do a great deal toward making her room beautiful. There is not one whose parents do not spend for her, on Christmas, and New Year's, and her birthday, a sum of money, more or less, which they would gladly give to her, if she preferred it, to be spent in adorning her room.

It is not at all impossible that her parents would like to give her, also, a small sum to be spent in ornamenting the common living-room of the house. This is really a work which daughters ought to do, and which busy, tired mothers would be very glad to have them do, if they show good taste in their arrangements. The girl who cares enough and understands enough about the expression of rooms to make her own room pretty, will not be long content while her mother's rooms are bare and uninviting, and she will come to have a new standard of values in the matter of spending money, as soon as she begins to want to buy things to make rooms pretty.

How much better to have a fine plaster cast of Apollo or Clytie, than a gilt locket, for instance! How much better to have a heliotype picture of one of Raphael's or Correggio's Madonna's, than seventy-five cents' worth of candy! Six shillings will buy the heliotype, and three dollars the Clytie and Apollo both!

No! It is not a question of money; it is a question of taste; it is a question of choosing between good and beautiful things, and bad and ugly things; between things which last for years, and do you good every hour of every day, as often as you look at them, and things which are gone in an hour or a few days, and even for the few days or the hour do harm rather than good.

Therefore I think it is right to say that it is the duty of every one to have his or her rooms cheerful and cosey, and, as far as possible, beautiful; the duty of every man and woman, the duty of every boy and girl.

To give minute directions for all the things which help to make rooms cosey and cheerful and beautiful, would require volumes. Many books have been written on the subject, and I often see these books lying on tables in very dismal rooms. The truth is, these recipes are like many recipes for good things to eat; it takes a good cook in the beginning, to know how to make use of the recipe. But there are some first principles of the art which can be told in a very few words.

The first essential for a cheerful room is — Sunshine. Without this, money, labor, taste, are all thrown away. A dark room cannot be cheerful; and it is as unwholesome as it is gloomy. Flowers will not blossom in it; neither will people. Nobody knows, or ever will know, how many men and women have been killed by dark rooms.

" Glorify the room! Glorify the room!" Sidney Smith used to say of a morning, when he ordered every blind thrown open, every shade drawn up to the top of the window. Whoever is fortunate enough to have a south-east or south-west corner room, may, if she chooses, live in such floods of sunny light that sickness will have hard work to get hold of her; and as for the blues, they will not dare to so much as knock at her door.

Second on my list of essentials for a cheerful room, I put — Color. Many a room that would otherwise be charming, is expressionless and tame for want of bright color. Don't be afraid of red. It is the most kindling and inspiring of colors. No room can be perfect without a good deal of it. All the shades of scarlet or crimson are good. In an autumn leaf, in a curtain, in a chair-cover, in a pin-cushion, in a vase, in the binding of a book, everywhere you put it, it makes a brilliant point and gives pleasure. The blind say that they always think red must be like the sound of a trumpet; and I think there is a deep truth in their instinct. It is the gladdest and most triumphant color everywhere.

Next to red comes yellow; this must be used very sparingly. No bouquet of flowers is complete without a little touch of yellow; and no room is as gay without yellow as with it. But a bouquet in which yellow predominates is ugly; the colors of all the other flowers are killed by it; and a room which has one grain too much of yellow in it is hopelessly ruined. I have seen the whole expression of one side of a room altered, improved, toned up, by the taking out of two or three bright yellow leaves from a big sheaf of sumacs and ferns. The best and safest color for walls is a delicate cream color. When I say best and safest, I mean the best background for bright colors and for pictures, and the color which is least in danger of disagreeing with anything you may want to put upon it. So also with floors; the safest and best tint is a neutral gray. If you cannot have a bare wooden floor, either of black walnut, or stained to imitate it, then have a plain gray felt carpet. Above all things, avoid bright colors in a carpet. In rugs, to lay down on a plain gray, or on a dark-brown floor, the brighter the colors the better. The rugs are only so many distinct pictures thrown up into relief here and there by the under-tint of gray or brown. But a pattern either set or otherwise, of bright colors journeying up and down, back and forth, breadth after breadth, on a floor, is always and forever ugly. If one is so unfortunate as to enter on the possession of a room with such a carpet as this, or with a wall-paper of a similar nature, the first thing to be done, if possible, is to get rid of them or cover them up. Better have a ten-cent paper of neutral tints and indistinguishable figures, on the wall, and have bare floors painted brown or gray.

Third on my list of essentials for making rooms cosey, cheerful, and beautiful, come — Books and Pictures. Here some persons will cry out: "But books and pictures cost a great deal of money." Yes, books do cost money, and so do pictures; but books accumulate rapidly in most houses where books are read at all; and if people really want books, it is astonishing how many they contrive to get together in a few years without pinching themselves very seriously in other directions.

As for pictures costing money, how much or how little they cost depends on what sort of pictures you buy. As I said before, you can buy, for six shillings, a good heliotype (which is to all intents and purposes as good as an engraving) of one of Raphael's or Correggio's Madonnas. But you can buy pictures much cheaper than that. A Japanese fan is a picture; some of them are exquisite pictures, and blazing with color, too. They cost anywhere from two to six cents. There are also Japanese pictures, printed on coarse paper, some two feet long and one broad, to be bought for twenty-five

cents each ; with a dozen of these, a dozen
or two of fans, and say four good helio-
types, you can make the walls of a small
room so gay that a stranger's first impression on entering it will be that it is adorned
for a festival. The fans can be pinned on
the walls in endlessly picturesque combina-
tions. One of the most effective is to pin
them across the corners of the room in over-
lapping rows, like an old-fashioned card-
rack.

And here let me say a word about corners.
They are wofully neglected. Even in rooms
where very much has been done in way of
decoration, you will see all the four corners
left bare, — forcing their ugly sharp right
angle on your sight at every turn. They
are as ugly as so many elbows ! Make the
four corners pretty, and the room is pretty,
even if very little else be done. Instead of
having one stiff, straight-shelved book-case

hanging on the wall, have a carpenter put triangular shelves into the corners. He will make them for thirty cents apiece, and screw them on the walls. Put a dozen books on each of the lower shelves, a bunch of autumn leaves, a pretty vase, a little bust of Clytie, or a photograph on a small easel, on the upper ones, and with a line of Japanese fans coming down to meet them from the cornice, the four corners are furnished and adorned. This is merely a suggestion of one out of a dozen of ways in which walls can be made pleasant to look at without much cost.

If the room has chintz curtains, these shelves will look well covered with the same chintz, with a plaited ruffle tacked on their front edge. If the room has a predominant color, say a green carpet, or a border on the walls of claret or crimson, the shelves will look well with a narrow, straight border of billiard-cloth or baize (to match the ruling color of the room) pinked on **the lower** edge, and tacked on. Some **people put on** borders **of gay colors,** in embroidery. **It is** generally **unsafe to** add these to **a room, but** sometimes **they have a** good effect.

Fourth on **my** list of essentials for a cosey, cheerful room, **I** put — Order. **This is a** dangerous thing **to say,** perhaps; but it is my honest conviction that **sunlight, color,** books and pictures come before **Order. Ob-** serve, however, that while it comes **fourth on** the list, it is *only* fourth; **it is by no** means last! **I** am not making **an** exhaustive list. **I do not** know where **I** should stop if **I** undertook **that. I am** mentioning only a few of **the first principles,** — the essentials. And in regard **to this very question of order,** **I am** partly at **a loss to** know how **far it is** safe to permit **it to lay** down its **law in a** room. **I** think **almost** as many rooms are spoiled by being **kept** in too exact order, **as**

by being too disorderly. There is an apparent disorder which is not disorderly; and there is an apparent order, which is only a witness to the fact that things are never used. I do not know how better to state the golden mean on this point than to tell the story of an old temple which was once discovered, bearing on three of its sides this inscription: "Be bold." On the fourth side the inscription: "Be not too bold."

I think it would be well written on three sides of a room: "Be orderly." On the fourth side: "But don't be too orderly."

I read once in a child's letter a paragraph somewhat like this:

"I look every day in the glass to see how my countenance is growing. My nurse has told me that every one creates his own countenance; that God gives us our faces, but we can make a good or bad countenance,

13

by thinking good or bad thoughts, keeping in a good or bad temper."

I have often thought of this in regard to rooms. When we first take possession of a room, it has no especial expression, perhaps, — at any rate, no expression peculiar to us ; but day by day we create its countenance, and at the end of a few years it is sure to be a pretty good reflection of our own.

BY STAGE TO BOSTON.

I HAVE been young, and now I have grown old,
    But never until yesterday I knew
How many living souls a stage can hold,
    And make the quickest time its journey through.

I came upon the stage so suddenly,—
    And, for a stage, in such a funny place;
I stood stock still, surprised as I could be,
    With blank amazement written in my face.

'Twas just behind old Deacon Thatcher's shed;
    The wheels in butter-cups sunk to the hubs;
The pole stretched over a white clover-bed,
    And almost into Mrs. Thatcher's tubs.

From every window looked out laughing eyes;
    From every window came a scream and shout;
Before, behind, the children swarmed like flies,
    And madly rocked the old blue stage about.

"O ho!" I said, and felt as young as they;
  "Whose stage is this?   To what town does it go?
And is there room for me to go to-day?
  And how much is the fare, I want to know?"

As quick as lightning all the children cried:
  "We go to Boston, and we've got our load;
But you can go if you will ride outside;
  The fare is just a dollar for each rod!"

"Oh dear!" said I, "your fare is much too high;
  The money that I have would not begin"—
"Jump on! jump on!" they all began to cry,
  "We'll take you once for nothing; you are thin!"

I knew much better than to spoil their fun;
  So I went on and found a shady place,
And watched, and saw that till the day was done
  They travelled tireless, at their quickest pace.

But all the time I watched I could not win
  My heart from thinking, while I dreamed and
      smiled,
Of that fair kingdom none can enter in
  Without becoming first a little child.

GOOD TEMPER.

THE dictionaries give eight definitions of the word "Temper"; some of them are rather surprising the first time one reads them. We are so in the habit of using words without thinking much about what they mean, that when we happen to look them out in the dictionary, we find that we are more ignorant than we supposed. The other day I was turning over the leaves of a dictionary, and my eye accidentally fell on a very common word, one we use every hour, of which I should have said that it might perhaps have half-a-dozen different meanings, and it had twenty-two! This shows you what an interesting book the dictionary is.

The second definition of the word "tem-

per " is, "the constitution or natural condition of the body." This is a definition
which we ought always to remember when
we are criticising other people's temper. It
ought to make us very charitable and very
patient. Nobody knows how much of the
ill-temper in the world is the result of a
feeble or diseased body. On the other hand,
however, nobody knows how much can be
done in the way of controlling the ill-temper
which is the result of a feeble or diseased
body, and therefore I think while we ought
to remember this definition when we are
judging other people, we would better forget it when we are judging ourselves. No
doubt that we will find plenty of excuses for
being cross, without going to the dictionary
for them. And yet, if one looks at the
matter honestly, is there really ever such a
thing as an excuse for being cross? Why,
the minute you sit down in a leisurely and

good-natured way, and think the thing over, does it not seem the stupidest thing in the world ever to permit one's self to give way to bad temper? In the first place, it never does the least good; on the contrary, it always makes bad matters worse. In the second place, it is misery. I don't believe there is anything in the world, except the toothache, which is so uncomfortable; and even the toothache doesn't make one look so hideous; no, not even if it swells one's cheek up to twice the natural size. A good-natured smile could make even such a face as that look not unpleasing; but a face distorted by bad temper nothing can redeem; and the worst of it is, that the distortion lasts. Every time a fit of bad temper happens, it leaves its mark behind it; there is no writing plainer than it writes on faces; day by day the lines grow deeper, as if they were graven in by a sharp instrument: ugly furrows between the eyes; a still uglier droop to the corners of the mouth! Why, even the babies know the face of a cross person, at sight, and begin to cry if he offers to touch them. Animals know it; cats and dogs run when they see some persons coming towards them; and, if you look closely, you will usually see that the person has some of the signs of bad temper on his face.

But I think I hear a whisper from some child who is reading this page, "Why, she said she was going to talk about 'Good Temper,' and she is speaking of bad temper all the while." So I am; and I wonder if I did begin my talk wrong-end foremost? No! I think not. I think the best way to understand what Good Temper is, is by observing bad temper: the best way to realize how much more sensible and comfortable a good-tempered person is, is to observe how silly and wretched bad-tempered people are.

It is much easier to define Good Temper by giving a list of the things it will never do, than by trying to tell what it does. And that would be the best way, too, to manufacture a recipe for Good Temper, I think: to mention all the things which must be left out, though this does really sound like an Irish Bull. Many people suppose that good temper and natural amiability are the same things. It is not so. Some of the best-tempered people I ever knew, were not naturally amiable at all; and I have several times in my life seen people who were called very amiable, who did not seem to me at all good-tempered. The sort of person who is generally called "very amiable," is apt to be very obstinate; and obstinacy is a trait of which a really good temper must not have a trace. Good Temper

must be ready to "give up"; give up having
its own way; give up trying to convince
other people that its own way is best; give
up having "the last word." How hard it
does seem, sometimes, to do this! how very
provoking it is to see a thing distinctly yourself, and not be able to make the person who
is disputing with you see it! And, if he
loses his temper, and says things which you
know that he must know are unjust, how
very hard it is to give up the argument, and
let the whole thing go. No! I used the wrong
word. I said, how hard it "is"! I ought
to have said, how hard it "seems." It is
not really half so hard in the long run, as
the other way, if we could only realize, at
the time, how little we should care about
the whole thing a few hours later; and how
much happier we should be by that time, if
we stopped short in the quarrel.

I suppose more bad temper is shown, and

more angry resentment felt, in disputes about
little things which are not really of the least
consequence, than in all other ways put together: about a date, for instance, or the
place where a thing was left; or the heat or
the cold, or the best way of doing something.

You have all seen people lose their tempers
sadly, in discussing trifles like these. Now
isn't it silly? In a week, in a day, perhaps,
we would not even remember the thing we
were quarrelling over; and if we did remember it, it would only be to be ashamed
of having allowed ourselves to be angry
about it.

This is a thing which good temper will not
do. Good Temper is too strong and too sensible; Good Temper thinks in time, and says
to itself, "Never mind; it is not of the least
consequence, one way or the other. Let it
go."

There is another thing which Good Temper thinks in time about: and that is about the sort of answer it is best to make to unkind or harsh words.

There is a little verse in the Bible which Good Temper has always at its tongue's end, as you might say:

" A soft answer turneth away wrath."

Good Temper will not let itself be provoked into "answering back." When people are too unreasonable or cross, so that even soft answers seem to do little good, Good Temper keeps silent; not a sulky silence — that is the worst possible shape which the worst possible temper can take — but a calm, gentle silence, ready at a second's notice to speak pleasantly about something else, as if nothing had happened.

There is one more thing which Good Temper does not do: it does not grumble. It is the easiest thing in the world to get a habit of grumbling, so many things go wrong every day, and every hour. I suppose there is not a person in this world, at this minute, who has not some real troubles, and a great many discomforts. And if we all lifted up our voices, and told them, there would be a great chorus of complaints. But Good Temper knows better. Good Temper holds its tongue: Good Temper has a shrewd old motto about such things, —

"What can't be cured must be endured."

These three things, then, Good Temper never does: never disputes, never answers back hastily, never grumbles. These are the negatives of its laws.

The things that it does, Time would fail us to tell, for they are so many; and they are not alike in any two people, in any two places. Good Temper is unselfish, likes to see other people comfortable. Good Temper helps everybody it can. Good Temper smiles when it looks into people's faces, and says a pleasant word whenever it has a chance. In short, Good Temper keeps the "Golden Rule," that wonderful, simple, short rule in so few words, which covers every act that is possible in the life of a human being.

The sixth definition which the dictionary gives of " Temper," is, —

" State to which metals, particularly steel, are reduced, in respect to hardness or elasticity."

The word elasticity here is the one which applies both to the temper of metals, and of men. Of the finest-tempered steel a weapon can be made so elastic that you may bend it double and it will not snap. The instant the pressure is removed it will fly back to its original shape, unbent, untarnished, and unhurt. This is wonderfully like the way the finest-tempered people meet the trials and crosses of everyday life. Good Temper bends double, if need be; but it does not snap. When the pressure is over, it is itself again as shining and perfect as ever. It is like the famous cimeter of Saladin, which put to shame King Richard's huge broadsword in the hands of King Richard himself. The broadsword was of good metal, no doubt; and it was "so long that it reached well nigh from the shoulders to the heels" of a man, the old tale says. Few men could even lift it; but Richard Cœur de Lion made nothing of swinging it round his head, and bringing it down with a blow that would fell an ox. One day, when he was in Palestine, to show the Saracens what he could do with this broadsword, he cut a thick bar of iron through, at a single stroke; the two pieces rolled on the ground, "as a woodsman would sever a sapling," and "the

blade of the sword was so **well-tempered as**
to exhibit not the least token of having
suffered by the feat it had performed."

Then Saladin, the Saracen Prince, took a
silken cushion stuffed with down, and plac-
ing it upright, asked **King** Richard if he
could cut that in two.

"No, surely," replied the King, "no sword
on earth can cut that which opposes no
steady resistance to the blow."

Ha! ha! how the Saracen must have
laughed when he heard the King say that,
for he knew very well that his cimeter,
which was narrow and light as a reaping-
hook, could cut that bag of down much
more easily than King Richard had cut the
iron bar.

Then the story goes on to say, "He drew
the cimeter across the cushion, applying the
edge so dexterously, and with so little apparent effort, that the cushion seemed rather

to fall asunder than to be divided by violence."

King Richard's followers did not like to see this; and one of them exclaimed:

"It is a juggler's trick; there is gramarye in this."

That is just the way we feel sometimes when we see how stupid people, and inert people, and obstinate people, are managed, and set right, and kindled up by one person's good temper brought to bear on them. It seems almost like "gramarye."

When the Englishman said this, the Saracen Prince took a thin veil, and letting it fall across the edge of his cimeter, cut that also into two pieces, which floated away in the air. This was even more wonderful than the other. How stupid and coarse the mere brute force of the great broadsword seemed after this!

There are occasions, no doubt, when the

broadsword kind of temper is of use ; but they are rare. For the everyday needs of everyday life, for the little worries, and the little perplexities, for the silliness, and the stupidity, and the contrariness of people, the fine, and light, and elastic touch of Saladin's cimeter is a great deal better.

LIZZY OF LA BOURGET.

I TELL you the tale as 'twas told to me.
  'Tis a tale that I dearly love to tell;
The tale of Lizzy of La Bourget,
  Of faithful Lizzy, who ran so well.

This Lizzy of La Bourget was a mare;
  She was all snow white except two black feet;
Her sire was an Arab steed, coal black,
  Her dam was a Cossack pony fleet.

Her Arab blood made her tireless and strong,
  Her Cossack blood made her loving and true;
Oh! Lizzy of La Bourget could love
  As warmly as human beings do.

She followed her peasant master to work,
  Obeyed at a sign or call of her name;
All day she tugged at his cart or plough,
  And bounding at night she homeward came.

She was never groomed, but she shone like silk,
   And fattened well on the poorest fare;
She played with the children like a dog,
   And the children fed her with her share.

When the war broke out and her master went
   To fight with the French, good Lizzy went too:
And many a battle, night and day,
   She carried him bravely, safely through.

But at last there came a turn in the tide,
   For Lizzy and master, disastrous day;
The day on which a battle was fought,
   A bloody battle at La Bourget.

The cavalry regiment, horse and man
   Were caught in an ambush and hemmed in:
The Frenchman captured them every one,
   And held them, a ransom large to win.

The captors were tipsy; 'twas late at night;
   The foolish men drank because they were glad:
Alone, by a half-open casement low,
   Sat Lizzy's poor master, weary and sad,

When, sudden, he heard a sound that he knew;
　He could not mistake, it was Lizzy's neigh;
She had broken loose and was seeking him,
　Oh, brave, good Lizzy of La Bourget!

The captors were tipsy; they did not hear
　Their prisoner call " Lizzy " in whisper low;
They did not notice the joyous neigh:
　The first they knew, with one ringing blow

The casement was burst from its hinges strong,
　Their prisoner had leaped on·his good mare's
　　　back;
. And through the darkness he raced, he flew,
　With a hundred bullets on his track.

No bridle! no spur! But well Lizzy knew
　The life of her master lay in her speed,
She ran like a whirlwind, and paid to the shots
　No more than to summer raindrops heed.

No compass! no guide! Nought knew the Hussar
　Of right or left in his perilous way;
But safe, sure instinct his Lizzy had,
　She knew the road back to La Bourget.

All night and the most of a day she ran,
   She had no water, she was not fed;
And when she arrived at La Bourget,
   You well may think, she was almost dead.

But a shout arose from each man who saw
   Her dash into camp with her gallant stride,
And the General himself came out to see
   The horse and the master of such a ride.

The fight had been fierce, and many men won
   Great fame in the heat of that bloody day,
But long after they are forgotten all,
   The world will know Lizzy of La Bourget.

KICKING AGAINST PRICKS.

THE world is full of things that prick. There are nettles, and burdocks, and thistles, and rose-bushes, and raspberry-bushes, and blackberry-vines, which every child knows by sight. Then in the South, and out in the far West, where I live, at the foot of the Rocky Mountains, there are in addition to all these, more than a dozen different kinds of cactus which prick worse than anything else in the world; and there is a plant called Yucca, which has long leaves almost as narrow as a grass-blade, pointed at the end, and as stiff as a knife. Sometimes this is called Spanish Bayonet, because its leaves are as sharp as the point of a bayonet. They could run a long way into flesh if they were used as weapons. I presume there are a great many more things that prick that I never heard of. Probably no country is without them; I am sure we have enough of them in America.

How carefully we move about where such things are growing! How closely we look where we step! Everybody knows nettles, and will not go near a nettle-bed if he can help it. In picking raspberries and black-berries, how sharply we look out not to get scratched by the thorns; how often we see beautiful purple thistles, and say to our-selves: "Oh, dear! if thistles hadn't such sharp thorns on them, I would pick one." And as for roses, it has passed into a proverb about them, —

"No rose without a thorn,"

which means that hardly anybody ever picked a rose in his life without pricking his fingers! The only way to handle any of these things safely, is to wear very thick gloves, or else to take a pair of scissors and cut off all the thorns before you touch the stems.

This is a great deal of trouble; but not so much trouble as to have to pick thorns out of your flesh, and to bear the pain of their pricking. Some thorns are poisonous, and the pain lasts a long time. I knew a lady in Colorado who carelessly stepped on a prickly pear-plant, — that is a kind of cactus; it has flat round leaves about as large as the palm of your hand, and shaped something like a mitten with the thumb left off. These leaves are quarter of an inch thick, and are covered all over with little pricking points, as fine as the finest needles; these points are called spines; they are so fine you can hardly see one alone by itself, and it is almost impossible to get one out of your flesh if once it has sunk in. This lady

stepped on some of these leaves, and the
spines ran through her boot and her stock-
ing, and went so far into her foot she could
not pull them out. Her foot swelled, and
her whole leg swelled; for two weeks she
had to sit with her leg resting on a chair,
and suffered great pain all that time. Don't
you believe she was careful always after that,
when she walked on the plains where the
cactus grew?

And now what do you suppose is the
reason I am saying all these things about
different sorts of plants which prick? I'll
tell you. This is a little sermon, and all
this first part about the plants that prick, is
the text to it.

Now comes the sermon itself; and you
see if it doesn't "stick to its text" better
than some sermons do.

There are hundreds of things in life that are
just like these thorny leaves and stems that

prick. Every day we come across them, or
they come across us! Some of them are like
the nettles and burdocks, just mere torments,
to get away from if we can: ugly-tempered
people, and stupid, tiresome people; I think
the ugly-tempered people are like nettles;
how they do sting us and make us smart!
and the stupid, tiresome people are like
burdocks; how they do stick to us when we
want to shake them off! But most of the
things in life which prick us are like
the roses, and the raspberries, and the
blackberries; good things which we want,
beautiful things which we like to see, and
wholesome things which it is best for us to
have; but they all have thorns, and if we
don't take hold of them the right way, we
shall surely get pricked. I will mention
one of the things I mean, and you will think
of dozens yourselves:

Sleep, is one. Once I asked a little girl

what she disliked most of all things in this world, and she answered me, without stopping to think a minute, —

"Bed-time! bed-time's the thing I hate worst! Bed-time's the meanest thing in all the world!"

I didn't wonder much, for I remember very well how I used to hate to go to bed when I was a child. But if I had only known then, as I know now, that every hour I spent in sleep was helping to make me a strong, healthy woman, and giving my body a chance to grow to its full size, I wouldn't have hated it so. No, indeed; I would have gone to bed early every night, of my own accord, without anybody's having to coax or to drive me. I should have known that the more hours I spent sleeping, while I was a little child, the better time I should have when I grew up.

But little children cannot possibly understand this. They cannot believe it when their fathers and mothers tell them. So they have to be made to go to bed early, no matter how much they dislike it. Almost every day I see some child being dragged off to bed, by a nurse or a mother; and when I hear it crying, and screaming, and holding back, I say, —

"Oh, you foolish child, you are kicking against the pricks! How much harder you make it for yourself, as well as for everybody else."

Now, I wish every boy and girl that reads this would just try, for one week, going to bed when the regular time comes, without making any fuss about it. Take the bed-time just as you take the dinner-time, or the tea-time, or the breakfast-time, or something that is fixed and settled, and that is the end of it. Why, at the end of the week you won't think much about it; when seven o'clock comes, or eight o'clock, whatever your bed-time is, you will go, as a matter of course, and you'll see how much happier you'll be. You will save ever so many pricks! Try it!

And it would be just so with all the things which children have to do which they don't like to do and all the things which they want to do, and can't; all such things are things with pricks. If you fret and cry and tease, that is kicking against the pricks, and you get dreadfully hurt. If you say to yourself resolutely, —

"Well, it can't be helped. I've got to do it. I'll make the best of it!" That is taking hold of the thorns the right way, and saves all the scratches.

There is one more thing to be said about this kicking against pricks: It always leaves shocking marks on people's faces.

You can imagine how a boy's clothes

would look, if he had been in a bed of
nettles and brambles, and had just plunged
right through, kicking the thorny stems on
every side. Why, he would look like a
beggar! his clothes would hang in rags and
tatters; great pieces would have been torn
out and left behind.

Now, our faces are the clothes of our
souls; and the strange thing is, that the
soul's clothes always show what shape the
souls have. The body's clothes are quite
different. You can have clothes made for
the body which will quite conceal its shape;
it may be deformed and ugly to look at, and
yet good clothes, rightly made, can almost
cover up the deformity. But not so with the
face, which is the outside garment of the soul.

If you kick against the pricks of life,
every kick leaves its mark on your face;
and if you keep on kicking, that is, if you
keep on fretting, and whining, and teasing,

and making a fuss about things that can't be helped, by and by your face will be all full of ugly lines and marks which are just like the rags and tatters which would come on your clothes if you plunged through a bramble-bed every day.

And you can mend the clothes; but you can't possibly mend a face. The scowls and the frowns, and the discontented looks, all grow deeper and deeper, the older we grow; sometimes we see old men or women with faces so full of such marks, that we are almost afraid to speak to them.

"Oh, what a cross old man!" "What an ugly old woman!" we say.

These are the men and women who began, when they were children, to kick against pricks, and have never left off.

And this is the end of the little sermon about pricks.

Did it not stick to its text?

MY FIRST VOYAGE ROUND THE WORLD.

FOUR heads peeped over my shoulder,
  And four merry voices said,
"Oh, Aunty! tell us a story
  Of some journey you have made."

The lilac-bush at the window
  Nodded, and whispered: "You know
There's that one you took in my shadow
  Almost thirty years ago."

I nodded back to the lilac,
  "Good friend, your plumes are as curled
As when I took, in their shadow,
  My first voyage round the world.

"But I am so old and weary,
  I almost forget that sail;
If I find I cannot tell it,
  Will you finish me the tale?"

15

The lilac-bush shook with laughter,
  And the fragrance floated in;
The children crowded up closer,
  And shouted: "Begin, begin!"

.

" Well, once there was a little girl."
                    "That's you,"
They cried.   " Yes, it was I, but 'twill not do
For you to interrupt.
                    " One day in June
She and her brother took their books at noon
And sat down on the grass, where lilacs made
A green and purple tent with pleasant shade.
They meant to study, but the day was hot;
And watching birds and bugs, they soon forgot
The lessons, and began to idly trace
With pencil-marks the atlas's old face.
But presently, with slow and sleepy gait,
As if they never heard of being late,
Two caterpillars crawled up on the map,
And stopped, and snuffed, and made their feelers
      snap
With wisest look, on land and on the sea.
' Halloo! old fellows,' cried the boy.   ' You'll be

Two travelled worms, and you shall draw our
    ships.
Go faster, now, or you shall feel the whips.'
Just then two dainty apple-blossoms blew
Down in their laps: one pink, one white. 'And
.   you
Shall be our ships.' he cried; 'one called "The
    Rose,"
The other, "Snow-bird."'

                "Then his sister chose
'The Rose' for hers; and with fine silken strings
They made the caterpillars, helpless things,
Fast to the ships, then watched to see them start.
Oh! ne'er before did worms play such a part;
Oh! ne'er before such ships go gliding through
The seas.   Each child a curving stamen picked
From out a tiger-lily bud, and pricked
The sluggish caterpillars right and left
Until they must have been of sense bereft,
If any sense they had.

           "'Oh! now I know
What I will do; for gold and pearls I'll go
To Africa; the good "Snow-bird" shall fly
Past all these islands,' said the boy.

" ' And I

Will carry first a whole ship-load of bread
To these poor Irishmen who are half dead
With famine,' said the girl; 'then through the
    Straits
Of old Gibraltar I will seek the gates
Of Thebes. Oh, dear! all of the River Nile
My caterpillar covers up. Don't smile,
Bad boy; yours is as much too big, and more,
To get between Madeira and the shore.
The open ocean is a better place
For ships towed at a caterpillar's pace.
I'm going round the world, like Captain Cook:
Here is the very track marked out he took.'
' And so will I,' cried he; ' see who will win:
The ship that without cheating first gets in
Shall be the champion ship.'

" Then hard and fast

The poor worms' legs were pricked. They hurried
    past
Whole continents in seconds. Side by side
These funny racers crawled. No time nor tide
Made odds to them: they thought but of escape.
At last, just as the ' Snow-bird' round the Cape
Of Good Hope turned, lo! in a fuzzy ball

Her caterpillar rolled him up, and no
Amount of pricks and shoves could make him go
Another step, or straighten out. The race
Was over, but 'The Rose' kept on apace;
Poor caterpillar! patient o'er and o'er
Cook's track in seventeen seventy-three and four,
Through Artic seas and past firm fields of ice,
Past tropic isles, where trade-winds load with
     spice,
He toiled. At last the play grew dull. 'The
     Rose'
Went into port; the 'Snow-bird' too; then those
Young tyrants set their victims free; more dead
Than live, the puzzled worms, with feeble tread,
Stole off, and ever after were esteemed,
No doubt, in their own country, as beseemed
Such travellers.

              "As for the girl and boy,
They grew up just like all the rest, through joy
And grief, 'with books, and work, and healthful
     play;'
But always they remembered well this day;
And when they journeyed in good earnest, said,
Sometimes with pensive laugh: 'That trip we
     made

By map, beneath the lilac-bush, was best;
No noise, no smoke, no cinders **to molest**
On land; no stormy gales on any sea;
Rivers **and roads, hotels and** harbors free;
Each step of that we both remember yet,
While last year's jaunts we jumble and forget.
Oh! sweet, wise days, when caterpillars made
Fast time enough for us 'neath lilac's shade;
And fancy was so strong that we took trips
Round the whole world in apple-blossom ships.' "

Four mouths stretching **round my shoulder,**
Put sweet **kisses on my lips;**
" Oh! Aunty, what funny stories!
How jolly **about the** ships! "

And just then a caterpillar,
Who had **listened** to each word,
Tumbled **down, quite blind** with terror,
Into the **mouth of a bird.**

And the lilac-bush at the window
Nodded at me with a laugh,
And whispered: "You're growing so old
You've forgotten more than half."

"A GOOD TIME."

HOW often we hear the phrase. It is in everybody's mouth; grown people's as well as children's. I think there is no other phrase we hear half so often. "Did you have a good time?" "Come and see us; we'll have a right good time!" "What shall we do for a good time, to-day?" "Oh, what a good time we have had!" or, "Dear me, we haven't had a bit good time!" Are not countless such sentences as these heard on every side, every hour of every day?

Everybody wants to have a good time, all the time, day in and day out. Hardly anybody does have a good time, so much of the time as that. Almost everybody's good times come once in a while: an afternoon,

or an evening, or a day; or sometimes, perhaps, a great treat of a week, or a month,
spent on a visit or a journey.

Some people would say that it is selfish
and silly to be all the while wanting to have
a good time; that we ought to just do our
duty, and not mind whether we have a good
time or not. I do not think so. I think it
is only natural to want to have a good time;
nobody can help liking to have a good time.
A person who says he doesn't care about it,
has something out of order in him some-
where, in his body or his soul: either he is
ill, or he is a hypocrite. It is not only
natural to want to have a good time, it is
sensible; could anything be sillier than to
let ourselves be uncomfortable, and miserable, and forlorn, if we can help it? Why
should we?

But we must stop a minute, and make sure
what we mean by the words "a good time,"

before we go any farther. Once I heard a little boy say, —

"I'm going to have a jolly good time, this afternoon!" and I said to him, —

"What is 'a good time,' Freddy?"

He looked at me for a few minutes without speaking. Then he said, —

"Ponds, and fishes in 'em, and lots of grasshoppers for bait."

That was the particular kind of good time he was going to have, that afternoon.

Another time, I asked a little girl the same question. She had just come to the house where I was stopping, and had asked two other little girls who lived there to come and spend the afternoon with her.

"Oh, do let them come!" she said to the little girls' mother. "Do! do! We'll have a real good time."

"What will you do?" I asked.

"We're going berrying," she replied. "The pasture's just full of blueberries."

Now do you think it was really the fishes or the blueberries which made the good time? Not a bit of it!

Sticking grasshoppers on a hook is a disagreeable thing to do, and leaning over the edge of a boat by the hour at a time makes any boy's back ache; and as for picking berries off low bushes, in a field where the sun shines hot as it does in July, it is just as tiresome a thing as one could find to do. No! The "good time" was in this: that catching the fishes, and seeing how many they could catch before supper-time, and trying hard to fill their pails with blueberries before it was time to go home, would make the time pass so pleasantly to the children, that it would be sundown before they would think it was more than the middle of the afternoon; and they would wish they

could have another afternoon joined right
on, without any night between. This was
the one secret of their good time, — being
busy.

Even if it is being busy with things which
it would be better not to do, it still makes
people have a certain sort of good time;
young people, for instance, who dance all
night, till they are tired out; or old people
who play cards half the night; and middle-
aged people who play billiards, or cricket,
or race in yachts, or with horses. What
everybody is seeking after is something
which shall keep him from being idle.
There is a dreadful phrase which you often
hear among people who have not enough
to do, — it is "passing time away;" "killing
time," also, they sometimes call it. Isn't
that a terrible expression to come from the
lips of a human being, who will not have, at
the outside, more than seventy or eighty

years' of time? not half enough to do all
that a man or woman ought to want to do
in this world !

"Killing time!" Killing is a very true
word there, for it is like a wicked murder
to waste time.

All these expressions show how strong
the desire is, in everybody, to have a good
time ; and that everybody has an instinct
that the way to have a good time is to have
always something to do.

.Now the mistake that most people make
about it is, that they think the "something
to do" must be provided for them by somebody else; must be forced upon them, as
you might say. They are to sit still and
wait, as if this life were a sort of great
tea-party, where occupation and amusement
were to be passed round like refreshments,
and it would not be polite to do anything
but wait quietly till your turn came to be

helped. I see crowds of people everywhere, who are really doing this absurd thing, though they don't know it. These are the people that you often hear say of a place, —

"Oh, it is a frightfully dull place," or of a summer or a winter that they have just passed, —

"It has been such a stupid summer," or "It was a stupid winter; nothing going on."

Sometimes, when I hear people saying such things as these, I wonder that God does not punish them instantly for their ingratitude to Him. I am sure if any earthly king had fitted up a place half as beautiful as this world, and half as full of lovely things to see, and wonderful things to learn, and had given it to a few men and women for their own, and then they were to walk up and down, and sit about, lazy and sleepy, and complain that it was "dull," and "stupid,"

the king would turn them all out pretty
quick. Wouldn't he? He would say, —

" You are a good-for-nothing set of vaga-
bonds. I think you must be idiots. You
do not deserve anything but a desert to live
in ; and it would not be a bit too hard punishment for you to have your eyes put out
and your hands cut off, if you will not use
them to any purpose. Clear out ! Clear
out ! I won't have you here. I'll find some
other kind of beings to put in my world."

Now the truth is, there is not a "dull"
spot on this earth, not one ; and there ought
not to be a "dull" moment in any human
being's life, not one. The barrenest place
you can find, has enough in it for a man to
study for his whole lifetime, and then he
wouldn't have learned all that could be
learned about it. You can sit down anywhere you like out of doors, and even
within reach of your hand there will be

more things than you can count, that you
do not know anything about; things that
you could not understand without having
studied at least half-a-dozen different sciences.
Why, it is enough to make us unhappy, just
to look closely down at any one square inch
of ground, at the little grains of earth, the
blades of grass, the weeds, the strange live
creatures it holds, and think how little we
know about them; and then, to think that if
we brought a good strong microscope and
put it above that square inch of ground, we
should discover hundreds more of growths
and living creatures too small to be seen by
our poor eyes, and much more wonderful
than the things they can see.

Now isn't it a strange thing that anybody
should ever call any place "dull" on such an
earth as that? Isn't it strange that anybody
can help having "a good time" here?

I think the more natural thing would be

for us to be half ready to cry, all the time, because there is so much to see, so much to do, so much to learn, that there isn't one-quarter time enough in any one day, and not half days enough in the longest lifetime.

One great trouble about people's having "a good time" is, that they do not begin young enough to form the habit of providing it for themselves. When I hear boys or girls say to their mother —

"What shall I do next?" I always think to myself, "Dear me! what a pity! Why doesn't their mother make them find out for themselves what to do?"

There is not a boy who cannot keep busy, if he tries, not a girl who cannot find plenty to do, if she likes, in-doors and out-doors, daytimes and evenings; there are more things to be looked at, more books to be read; more things to be contrived and made by fingers, than any boy or girl can get through

with, before childhood is over, and manhood
and womanhood begin. Almost every child
has some one thing it likes best to do. I
know a boy who has a passion for bugs;
it keeps him hard at work all the time he
can get out of school; in the summer he
catches every winged creature he can find;
in the winter he arranges them, and studies
about them; he has already a collection
which any naturalist might be glad to own,
and in the hours he has spent out of doors,
he has learned a great many other things
about nature besides what he knows about
bugs. That is one of the most beautiful
and wonderful things about knowledge: that
no one bit of knowledge is alone by itself;
it has others which are so closely connected
with it, that if you know one well, you are
sure to know the others; just as if you
know a person very intimately, you are
pretty sure, sooner or later, to know his

16

brothers and sisters, and even his aunts and uncles and cousins. It is quite likely that this boy will be a great naturalist when he grows up; that is, he will devote his whole life to studying the earth and the creatures that live on it. But even if he does not, if he becomes a business-man, or a doctor, or a lawyer, he will be happier all his. life for knowing about bugs. When he goes into the country, he will never find it "dull." Every corner of the fields will be full of interest to him, and he will help his own boys have "a good time," just as he used to have it when he was a boy himself.

I know a little girl, too, who has a love for making little dishes out of clay. She makes little bowls, and pitchers, and plates, and then she paints stripes or figures of gay colors on them; she has quite a little china-shop of her own. When other children would be asking, perhaps, what they should do, or what game they should play, Caddie sits down and makes a new wash-bowl and pitcher for her baby-house,

Now I don't mean, by telling you these stories, to make you think that all boys must catch bugs, or all girls make clay pitchers; only that each child ought to find some one thing it likes best, and spend time enough on it to do it well; you can do one thing one year, and another thing the next year, perhaps: make a collection of bugs one summer, and of flowers the next; draw one winter, and paint the next; it is not so much matter what it is, so long as you care enough about it to like to do it, and to keep at it till you do it as well as it can be done; or at least as well as it can be done by you. When you love any one thing, like this, you will always have it in your own power to have "a good time;" no place can be "stupid" to you; no day "dull," and the chances are that you will in many ways get a great deal of good out of this one thing you can do. Somebody said once, " a man will always, make his way in life if he can do any one thing better than anybody else can do it ; if it is only making a toothpick ! "

And I think it was Dr. Johnson who said that happiness had only these ingredients :

1. Health.

2. A little more money than you need.

3. A little less time than you want.

"A little less time than you want?" That means, always to have so many things you want to see, to have, and to do ; that no day is quite long enough for all you think you would like to get done before you go to bed.

This is the one great secret of " A Good Time," and it is a secret which never wears out. This kind of " good time " lasts as long as you live.

SEA AND SHORE.

A Poetical Selection.

Square 18mo. *Cloth, red edges.* *Price* $1.25.

"The table of contents of 'Sea and Shore' would captivate Neptune himself, if he reads English. No one who has fitly sung the praises of his kingdom has been left out. . . . It seems impossible to find a good short poem about the sea, in all English literature, that is not included in this captivating collection. . . . And to take the volume into the country will be as good as taking a small poetical library." — *The N.Y. Tribune.*

"We are full of the poetry of the ocean to-day, having been inspired by the most charming little volume bearing the title at the head of our article. We merely invite attention to the book, which is a graceful tribute to that love of the sea which we all have at some time felt. We shall not say by whom it is made, for Messrs. Roberts Brothers do not; but we think that Mrs. Goddard and Miss Harriet W. Preston might tell us, if they would." — *Arthur Gilman, in Boston Transcript.*

"The 'Sea and Shore' is a small flexible volume that can easily be carried in one's pocket, yet it contains specimens of the sea poetry of many lands and many centuries. The book is beautifully executed, and many will find it a most attractive companion in their sea or mountain revels." — *Boston Daily Advertiser.*

Sold everywhere. Mailed, postpaid, by the Publishers,

ROBERTS BROTHERS, Boston.

SOME WOMEN'S HEARTS.

By LOUISE CHANDLER MOULTON.

16mo. Price $1.50.

"The title of the book which Mrs. Moulton now sends forth is not descriptive of a single story filling the whole volume, but is the ribbon which binds together in one volume eight stories of various length. The title proves to be something more than an external ligature. It is the hint of a connection that is far deeper, and that groups these stories into each other's company for the very good reason that they are really of kin. They tell the heart-history of women who have had to accept in this life some large portion of temptation, adversity, and sorrow, and have been faithful and true, and have gained the victory. . . . Mrs. Moulton has the incommunicable tact of the story-teller. She sees with the certainty of instinct what belongs to a story and what does not; has the resolution to sacrifice whatever is incongruous; adjusts the narrative in a sequence that arouses expectation from the start and holds it to the end. We find, also, in these novelettes, a quality which characterizes all her writings in this kind, — not merely artistic perfection in form, but artistic unity in substance. Each story of hers is complete, and each is single. A severe logical law controls each, — a law which makes these stories seem a growth, and not a manufacture. Each is as perfect in this unity as a Greek tragedy or a sonnet of Petrarch's. There is no 'moral' appended to any; yet the moral of every one is so interwoven with its texture, and so inevitable a part of it, as to make its impressiveness at times overwhelming." — *Christian Union.*

"The groundwork of these stories betrays a rare insight into the mysteries of human emotion." — *The N. Y. Tribune.*

"Taken as a whole, there is hardly a better collection of short stories by an American writer in print." — *The Literary World.*

"A bouquet of as graceful and fragrant stories as were ever bound up together." — *The Golden Age.*

Sold by all Booksellers. Mailed, postpaid, by the Publishers,

ROBERTS BROTHERS, Boston.